TSARDUST

TSARDUST

Kathleen Everett Upshaw
and
Howard Dean Everett

iUniverse, Inc.
New York Lincoln Shanghai

Tsardust

iUniverse, Inc.

For information address:
iUniverse, Inc.
2021 Pine Lake Road, Suite 100
Lincoln, NE 68512
www.iuniverse.com

ISBN: 0-595-29920-2 (pbk)
ISBN: 0-595-66079-7 (cloth)

Printed in the United States of America

CHAPTER 1

▼

Upon returning to the *Queen Anne*, Jon Olsen found an urgent message from his Aunt Violet. He had spent a fruitless morning searching for his cousins in Helsinki—a task Violet had pressed upon him before he left the United States—and the tone and content of her message troubled him more than the missing cousins.

Aunt Violet informed him that she would be in Norway by the time the note reached his ship, and that he was to abandon the cruise when it reached Oslo in order to help her conclude some urgent business. No further explanation was offered, leaving him perplexed as well as concerned.

It was not so much that Jon minded leaving a Baltic-Sea cruise still in its first week. After all, the ship had proved less luxurious—and far more crowded—than the brochures had promised, and the stormy crossing from Stockholm had left him almost queasy, a feeling that had not entirely subsided after a day of wandering the streets of Helsinki. No, it was the letter that gave him pause. For one thing, it was dated only two days earlier—June 18. Since mail from the States could not possibly have reached him so quickly, he concluded that Aunt Violet had misdated it. She frequently demonstrated eccentricity of one sort or another, but Jon could hardly imagine falling victim to so great an eccentricity as total disregard of time and its passage.

Stranger still was the final sentence of the note, which sounded oddly like a warning. "Do not try to contact me from St. Petersburg," Aunt Violet had written, the words heavily underlined and in her large script. At least Jon assumed the script was hers. The few other letters he had received from her had been typed, as nearly as he could recall. Perhaps on this occasion Violet had been away from her Virginia home, without access to a computer or typewriter. He took the envelope and looked for a postmark. To his surprise, it was from Helsinki, the city in which his ship was presently berthed!

In his deliberate way, Jon sought to account for this oddity. He and Violet had cousins in Helsinki—Rudi and Xenia Anderson. They were the very relatives Jon had missed seeing today. Had Violet flown into Helsinki before Jon arrived and persuaded Rudi and Xenia to accompany her to Oslo? If so, that explained his failure to find the couple at home this afternoon, despite prior arrangements. It also explained the postmark.

On the other hand, Aunt Violet could have simply written to Rudi and Xenia and enclosed the note to Jon for them to forward when his ship docked in Helsinki. In which case, not finding the couple home suggested nothing more or less momentous than a change in plans. Perhaps they were vacationing, as he had at first suspected, or perhaps something had come up in connection with their jewelry business. Good manners, of course, would seem to require that the couple notify Jon of such a change in plans, but it all went back to the matter of family eccentricities, he supposed.

Unperturbed by his cousins' thoughtlessness, Jon made his way to the smaller lounge on the main deck. From a table there he could observe the passengers returning along the wharf from their day's activities. Because the ship had docked around a corner, as it were, from the primary harbor, the view of Helsinki's skyline was less than satisfying.

He felt sorry for the travelers who had stayed on board today, since Helsinki had proven so interesting architecturally and geographically. Back home in St. Paul he made his living as a civil engineer, so he enjoyed examining and mulling over the layouts of unfamiliar towns and cities. It was fascinating to delve into their elevations and construction oddities, for example. Such explorations constituted a primary attraction in all his travels.

Ordering a vodka and tonic, he turned his thoughts from Helsinki and the passengers to his aunt's letter, which he understood only partially. The gist of the message, that Jon stay in Oslo once the ship put in there, remained obscure as to causes and implications. "Someone will meet you," she wrote. Yet the absence of all explanation made even so concrete a statement sound basically vague.

He believed he understood Aunt Violet's injunction against calling from St. Petersburg. Her grandfather, Peter Strasser, had done business in Russia following the revolution of 1917. A rich and influential man, he had known both Trotsky and Lenin. Such ties had permitted him to escape his Russian entanglements with his fortune intact. The Bolsheviks had allowed him to flee with a notable collection of ikons, woodcarvings, and Faberge jewelry. In return for his freedom, they confiscated his Russian business.

The Russian collection proved quite valuable in the long run, although the Strassers today owned very little of it. During the Great Depression, Aunt Violet's father, Henrik Strasser, had been forced to sell numerous objects from his collection—at prices far below their earlier and subsequent value.

At least partly as a result of this family history, Jon knew that Aunt Violet mistrusted anything and everything Russian. He had heard the old woman rail against the Bolsheviks as well as the Soviets, branding both as a "gang of criminals." Any political party that succeeded Nicholas and Alexandra—her beloved Tsar and Tsarina—was anathema in Violet's eyes. Thus presumably she forbade Jon to call from St. Petersburg—which was the *Queen Anne*'s next stop on its Baltic itinerary—lest his telephone be tapped. Alternately, Violet may simply have sought to deprive the Soviets of even so small a revenue.

However that might be, Jon wondered if he ought not to call her now, from the ship. Six days would elapse before he emerged from Soviet territory—six days during which he'd be puzzling about what Aunt Violet wanted. With this idea in mind, he rose and left the lounge.

As he reached the grand staircase, a horde of Italian matrons, all gabbling at once in their seamless native tongue, were surging upwards. Jon was forced against the railing as they pushed by with total indifference to his existence, despite his commanding size.

He waited politely, then decided against following in their wake, though all before it gave way. Instead, he made his way to the outside deck and up a lesser staircase, which narrowed to almost nothing at the top. When he came to the communications room, its door stood open. Stooping and stepping partially across the threshold, he asked about making a transatlantic call before the ship left port. The communications officer shrugged, took his name and stateroom number, and asked where he would be the next half hour.

Replying that he would be on the foredeck, Jon dutifully went there, so living to regret his selection. A large group of Spanish teens arrived immediately and began playing volleyball with such energy and noise that they soon drove everyone except Jon away. A tall and slightly forlorn figure, he sat on a bench, his back turned to the game, and prayed unrealistically for temporary deafness, or at least a cold beer.

At the end of thirty minutes, having heard nothing from ship officials, he arose from his bench and returned to the communications room, to accost the same officer. This person at first seemed vague, but subsequently appeared to recollect. "All channels taken," he said. "Six hour wait." Retreating, Jon had a nagging doubt the officer had made any effort at all.

The trouble was, the cruise had been over-booked by almost 15 percent. The steamship line blamed this excess on an unusually large number of families with children. The French and American passengers agreed with that explanation, as there definitely was a plethora of

Italian and Spanish tots. They got under foot like unfed cats. They materialized everywhere they should not: in bars, at floorshows, beside the roulette wheel. This ubiquity produced at times a nightmarish quality, particularly affecting the French.

"What insanité, what horreur!" a middle-aged French lady had confided to Jon on the second day out as they plowed from Amsterdam to Stockholm. She had almost nothing covering her ample self—a little patch across each well-developed breast and another little patch down below—yet her moral sense clearly registered outrage at so many children in the ship's only pool. "Possibly zey will drown," she said hopefully. "Zey have so little supervision."

Jon and this Frenchwoman spoke comfortably together every day, without being aware of any novelty in their tolerance of each other—in spite of the general dislike between citizens of the two nations. Jon decided that Madame Perpignan, unlike so many of her countrymen, was not condescending because she was not a French intellectual and had not developed the insufferable affectations of that breed. On the other hand, he realized that something personal about him might have appealed to the Parisian: his air of calm, perhaps, or the unfathomable expression imposed on his face by the scar on his cheek.

Beyond Madame and the persons sharing his table each evening at dinner, Jon had made virtually no real acquaintances on the voyage thus far. Despite his commanding physique and piercing eyes, nobody had approached him in expectation of an intimate encounter—tales of quick and easy shipboard romances notwithstanding. Perhaps the women were all married, tied down by husbands and children. Perhaps his six-and-a-half-foot height and no-nonsense air put them off. Or maybe it was the scar on his cheek—an imperfection that didn't so much disfigure as wrap him in an aura of indefinable mystery. Whatever the reason, Jon gave no hint of noticing.

He would have taken the Finnish lake tour today, but for his expectation of meeting Rudi and Xenia in Helsinki. It promised much robust walking, which he loved and at which he excelled. He recalled watching the passengers boarding the buses that morning. He had envied them the brochure's promises: coniferous forests, charming inns, small hamlets—doubtless with the most challenging waste-disposal arrangements, he guessed. However, as he almost always gave duty a higher priority than pleasure, he set out for his relatives' house.

Although the cousins lived several miles from the *Queen Anne's* moorings, Jon had determined to walk the distance. Before leaving Amsterdam he had purchased a Helsinki map. He consulted the map from time to time, as he walked neither briskly nor sluggishly along a minor artery, through a park, past the Orthodox cathedral, across an interestingly constructed bridge, then through another park. Until reaching the cathedral, he saw almost no human beings except fellow tourists who, like himself, had elected to walk.

Across the bridge lay the main harbor and a marketplace, already alive with vendors and potential customers. Jon had taken time to saunter among the stands, to admire the scrupulously clean turnips and natural fox coats, so oddly juxtaposed. He also detoured to the edge of the docks, to see what he might learn about Finnish pier construction, before resuming his route. He passed through cultural enclaves, financial and retail districts, and housing of every sort. Everywhere there were architectural splendors and pleasantries and follies. Everywhere he proceeded along uncluttered streets lined with glistening facades, as though the Finns had constructed a sort of modern Oz for themselves.

When he reached Rudi and Xenia's address, he saw an elegant-looking apartment house in a nameless, contemporary style. Its most interesting feature was ornamental ironwork jutting from its structural beams, so producing an impact like that of snow on branches. The building rose directly at the sidewalk's edge, without relying on any kind of landscaping for its effect.

Jon entered and found himself in a large vestibule with a marble floor and walls of chrome and black mirrors. Along one side were ranged the names of tenants, each above a small chrome grill covering a mailbox, with a black button below. He looked for "Anderson" and pressed the button.

There was no response, so he rang again. After several minutes passed, he considered what course to pursue next, whereupon the inner vestibule door suddenly opened to admit a sleek and elderly matron.

Jon removed his sun hat—a large-brimmed, floppy straw he often used for fishing expeditions back home. "Pardon me," he said, "I was looking for the Andersons." Though he'd never met his cousins, he was sure, by reason of her age, that this lady was not Xenia.

She said several words to him, but they were unintelligible. Indeed, he could not even be sure of the language. He sensed, however, that the shabbiness of his hat together with his size provoked the mistrust, if not fear, he read in her face.

He tried to communicate a second time, but she burst forth in her incomprehensible tongue, looking pointedly at the hat in his hands. He could not imagine why, unless the Finns had some odd custom about when to remove hats.

"Anderson," he said, and pointed to the name on the mailbox. Then he gestured and grimaced in a way he hoped conveyed a question.

She squinted at the box. After a moment she repeated, "Anderson," followed almost immediately by several remarks made with very authoritative-sounding syllables. In fact, she had switched from Finnish to Swedish, and though Jon recognized the change, he understood this tongue no better than the other.

"You know where they've gone?" he asked, thinking this might be the message she intended. As visual aids, he pointed to the name Anderson, waved goodbye, and looked inquiringly at the ceiling, then returned his hat to his head and spread out his hands, palms up. He meant this sequence to convey general lack of knowledge, but he knew it might equally well be interpreted as, "Is it going to rain?"

The lady pronounced, very deliberately, "An-der-son. Cris-ti-an-ya." She looked up at him fixedly, to discover whether he understood.

He nodded. "To Cris-ti-an-ya? Ah."

She favored him with the faintest of smiles, then nodded with a regality that implied an earlier century or at least cultural superiority. She was, he saw, very old, but also very magnificent. Accordingly, he managed a quite acceptable bow as she passed him on her way to the outer door.

After her departure, he had accepted the idea that his relatives had gone to the lakeside resort of Christiania. They must have opted for a holiday by the Finnish lakes, just as he would have liked to do. He had heard much about summer in Finland from his mother and Aunt Violet. They spoke of the extended daylight, the primordial stillness, and the distant but specific threat of the Nordic winter.

He realized winter's threat was always there, underlying the picnics and early harvests. He'd seen the cold formation of the serried clouds, the lingering damage from last winter, the glaciated marks on the earth itself. Always there. But not necessarily unsettling to a confident visitor from America conversant with technical progress and the specific wonders of civil engineering.

Now, as he continued to ponder the happenings of today in the light of Aunt Violet's note, an unsettling thought struck him. The dignified old lady at Rudi and Xenia's was from Aunt Violet's generation. And to that generation Oslo would forever be known as Christiania. For three hundred years and well into the twentieth century, Oslo had been called by that name. What if the old lady had no more regard for the name "Oslo" than his aunt had for "Leningrad"?

If, indeed, the old lady was telling Jon that Rudi and Xenia had not gone to the lake district at all but were now in Oslo—presumably with Aunt Violet—this realization put a whole new light on things. He felt a vague unease as he wondered what circumstances might have drawn all the remaining members of his family to Norway.

CHAPTER 2

▼

Violet Strasser learned of Yelena Anderson's death just one month earlier, in May. The news came to her from a friend they had in common, Countess Dahlmark. According to the Countess, Yelena had died out-of-doors, "in a kind of meadow on Bygdøy." She did not mention the cause, possibly because Yelena was so old, having been born prior to the turn of the century.

Violet had seen Yelena only twice in her life, the first time in 1925. Though she was just eight years old at the time, Violet nonetheless remembered the meeting well—or at least a specific part of it—for it was the only time she had ever encountered a ghost.

In 1925 Mrs. Strasser had taken the girls—Violet and her older sister Hia—to Europe for the summer, to enhance their education. They did the Grand Tour and then some, so making up for visits prevented by the Great War. Immediately before traveling to Christiania to meet Mr. Strasser, they spent several weeks in London and Devonshire, where they were briefly presented to King George of England. Violet would not have remembered the encounter with Yelena but for the significance others attached to it.

Like most cities in the world, Christiania was smaller in 1925 than now. When the Strassers went to visit Yelena Anderson, they left the hotel on foot, because nowhere in Christiania lay far from anywhere else and because it was a beautiful day besides. Mr. and Mrs. Strasser walked arm in arm behind their girls, who were beribboned and pinafored and wearing white stockings and patent-leather shoes.

Violet had a marginal awareness that their destination involved Daddy's business in Russia—a place encased in ice except long enough to grow lilacs once a year. He'd been there all the time Mommy and Hia and she rode trains and looked at dark pictures in old castles and museums. He was in Russia doing business. His business involved meeting people, and making things, and selling them, just as he did at home in America.

Daddy had said that Hia and she wouldn't be bored when they got where they were going, that there would be lots of things to see at the Andersons—things like Imperial Easter Eggs and jewelry and clocks and miniatures. When he explained that miniatures were pictures, she made a face. She was tired of pictures.

Their walk took them through a beautiful park with a fountain, which Daddy said belonged to the King. The jet from the fountain shot high into the air, and in descent the droplets made rainbows, if you cocked your head way 'round and peeked under your left arm just exactly right and…

"Violet!" came her mother's voice, "what *are* you doing!"

When they reached the Andersons, they climbed a flight of stairs to the door. Under the windows, on either side, hung flower boxes, and bugs were eating some of the plants. When Violet leaned over the railing to watch the bugs, she caught one of her hair bows as she withdrew. So she entered the house with one bow askew.

Mr. Anderson wasn't there, which seemed a disappointment for Daddy, and Mrs. Anderson looked to be twenty at least or maybe even older. She made a fuss over Violet and Hia at first. But after showing them the cases of jewels and other pretty things, which reminded Violet of all those trips to museums, she put the girls in a corner with a wooden jigsaw puzzle.

Mommy and Daddy and Yelena—that's what they called Mrs. Anderson—began talking. They went on about all kinds of adult things, about Daddy's "collection" and Yelena's "connections." They mentioned that poor man called "the Tsar," whom Violet thought had been killed at a place called Sarajevo and somehow started the Great War. The Tsar had children who were murdered at another funny-sounding place. Violet heard Mrs. Anderson say the Tsar's whole household was shot, and only one escaped.

When Mrs. Anderson brought out a picture, Mommy said, "Girls! Come see Mrs. Anderson's miniature of the Tsar and Tsarina!"

Naturally Violet obeyed, although she resented leaving the puzzle depicting something called "The Althing." That appeared to mean a lot of men in furs. She peered over her mother's shoulder at the couple in Mrs. Anderson's miniature. Violet thought it looked like the king they met in England and a tiny bit like the same queen.

After this interlude, the girls were encouraged to return to their puzzle. Their daddy began talking to Mrs. Anderson about her Easter Eggs. They talked and talked, while Violet and Hia worked steadily at the puzzle. Violet heard them say the Eggs belonged to the Tsar and were older than creation. Mommy kept picking up one Egg that sparkled all the way across the room and saying how beautiful it was. Then she opened the top and withdrew a tiny golden bird that sparkled in different colors, at which the adults sighed and made the biggest fuss imaginable. After Mommy returned the bird to its Egg, Daddy began talking to Mrs. Anderson in Russian. At least, Violet thought it might be Russian.

She asked Hia in a whisper, "Is that Russian?"

"Yes!" Hia almost hissed in an effort to be both unobtrusive and explicit.

"Isn't Mrs. Anderson Norwegian?"

"No!" Hia whispered, her eyebrows drawn together in a frown of warning for her little sister.

Violet felt her ignorance profoundly. Thanks to Hia's superior knowledge of the world, Violet clearly saw how stupid it was to assume a woman living in Norway might be Norwegian. How dumb she remained at eight, despite dragging through all those museums and palaces! Very put out with herself, she stopped fitting the puzzle pieces and looked down at her hands.

It was then that the very odd, memorable thing happened. She was twiddling her thumbs and trying to think up ways of regaining face with Hia, when something prompted her to look up. She couldn't say what, exactly. It was just a feeling, as if someone watched her, or as if a shadow had moved toward her from the doorway.

And there, beyond the glass cases with their various ornaments and objects, just beyond the doorway, stood a bearded man, impeccably dressed, of military carriage, peering at her. He seemed to emanate light, to bathe and be bathed with light. He looked at her very seriously, very solemnly.

She tried to say her sister's name, but no voice, not even a whisper, came. Then she started to reach out to Hia, but she could not move a finger, much less her arm. The apparition meanwhile continued to regard her with dedicated, autumnal gravity, until it withdrew behind the jamb, its left foot being the last bit to disappear. Only then did she let out her breath, rather loudly.

Hia barely took notice of the sound, but the adults turned as one to look. For a brief moment all three gazed at Violet calmly, as upon an average sunset. Then Mrs. Anderson gathered herself up and hastened over. "Have you seen something, darling? Yes?" she asked, subsequently looking in the exact direction of the vanished ghost.

"What is it?" Mrs. Strasser seemed merely puzzled.

Mr. Strasser strode toward Violet. "All those chocolates?" he inquired. "Are you sick, dear?"

"Violet's not sick!" declared Hia, at the same time viewing Mrs. Anderson curiously.

Mrs. Anderson, who had knelt next to Violet and had put her arm around the girl's shoulders, now yielded her place to Mr. Strasser. As she rose and stepped back, she kept her eyes fixed on the doorway. Her complexion had paled.

Meanwhile Mr. Strasser picked up his younger daughter to inspect her. "Sure you're not sick?" he asked. Violet shook her head. When perfectly satisfied that she remained healthy, he put her down and returned to the other side of the room. Mrs. Anderson followed.

As soon as they were left to themselves, Hia whispered, "What was it?"

"Let's talk later!"

And although Hia mildly protested a delay, she abided by Violet's decision lest they attract too much attention. Not long after, a stir among the adults indicated the visit might be coming to an end. The two Strasser girls ceased matching puzzle pieces to watch saucer-eyed for indications of their imminent departure.

Later that night, when they were alone in their bedroom of the suite Mr. Strasser had engaged for his little family, the sisters took up the incident.

"Well, what did you see?" demanded Hia.

Violet told her it was either the man they met called King George or the Tsar. Hia protested that King George lived in England and the Tsar was killed at Ekaterinburg. For some minutes they sidetracked into debating where the Tsar met his death. Violet of course thought Sarajevo. Then they continued with the more vital topic of the apparition.

Hia, while doubting Violet's identification of the man seen, did not at all contest his presence. "Mrs. Anderson saw him too," she said in confirmation. Next she had the happy thought that the man might be Mr. Anderson, and that Mr. Anderson might be the Tsar. Maybe someone other than the Tsar was killed, like in the Alexander Dumas story.

"I don't know," demurred Violet, annoyed that her sister read and remembered so much.

"Mrs. Anderson said one member of the family escaped, when she was talking about the executions. Maybe the Tsar escaped!"

"And Mrs. Anderson's hiding him!" cried Violet, going along with enthusiasm. She looked at Hia in admiration. "That must be it!"

They went on to discuss whether Mrs. Anderson might be the Tsarina or whether the Tsar merely chose to go under an assumed name. They decided the latter must be the case, since Mrs. Anderson didn't look at all like the Tsarina in the picture. In this fashion, the sisters dealt practically with a matter whose nature made it impossible to do so.

Over the years, Violet from time to time looked back upon the incident. Indigestion or the Tsar's escape were two possible explanations for the apparition, but each failed to muster supporting evidence then or later. Occasionally she wondered if she might have suffered a moment's hysteria. After all, she was an imaginative child and had overheard all that talk about killings and mine shafts amidst the contrasting gorgeous examples of the Tsar's treasures.

Possibly, without going so far as hysteria, she had merely endowed a figure actually seen in Mrs. Anderson's house with the attributes of the Tsar. It was in fact odd that, while remembering the apparition's expression so precisely, she could not recall what he wore. Even the foot that disappeared last from her view—she could not positively say it was booted.

Circumstances, recollections, and reflection caused her ultimately to speculate that on that day so long ago, Mr. Anderson had returned to his house, had started into the drawing room, and had withdrawn at sight of Mr. Strasser, whom he did not wish to see. Such an explanation adequately accounted for Mrs. Anderson's reactions and left in doubt only Mr. Anderson's motivation.

Such was her preferred explanation, but she had lived sufficiently long to know how mysterious life is. Why, for example, had Yelena

Anderson refused to sell Henrik Strasser any of the "lost" Imperial Eggs? Why had the one man Violet ever loved failed to declare himself? The answers to such questions eluded capture like the might-have-beens the questions implied.

Of course, sometimes a mystery could be cleared up. More often, it faded from memory for lack of intrinsic glamor. One seldom concerned oneself more than a day with the strange disappearance of a grocery list or a labor racketeer. She wished all mysteries might be so—either solved or glamorless—for then one could be done with them. Then, at her advanced age, she wouldn't be wasting her time on something that occurred at the age of eight!

Unfortunately the apparition, Yelena, and the Tsar's treasures had become a major frustration in her life. So much so, in fact, that from the moment Violet learned of Yelena's death on Bygdøy, she sensed that the answers to the mysteries might be rapidly slipping away, if not already irrevocably gone.

And then, not a week after receiving notification of Yelena's death, Violet found an official-looking envelope in her mailbox. Writing from the United States Embassy in Oslo, Norway, Ms. Anna Nygaard advised Ms. Violet Strasser of Alexandria, Virginia, USA, that the addressee had been named an heir to the estate of Ms. Yelena Anderson, lately of Oslo. The said Nygaard's essential inquiry was: what did Violet propose doing about it?

CHAPTER 3

▼

Jon awoke to a stale stateroom with daylight slitting at the edges of the porthole drapes. He lay sluggish, disinterested, until the thought came to him that Soviet Russia must now lie outside his porthole. Energized, he sat up, drew back the drape, and stared out at a great panorama of drab concrete. Evidently this was what the Soviet Union had become in 1983.

He beheld a wide concrete quay, concrete pillars supporting a concrete slab, and a concrete wall with interstices through which one could see a concrete walk and drive. There was no movement whatsoever: no people, no vehicles, not even a flapping Soviet flag—at least, not within Jon's view. Visually bored, he turned away to begin his morning routine.

Later, arriving on deck for breakfast, he spotted Madame Perpignan at a table by herself. She permitted him to join her, and as he took his seat, he looked again toward land and this time saw a red flag with a gold hammer and sickle. It hung limp on its flagpole, prominent atop the concrete slab.

"I zee a hot day ahead," Madame predicted resignedly.

"Which tour are you taking?"

"Leningrad," she replied. "And you?"

"The same. Perhaps we'll be together."

"Non. Zey have a French bus, maybe two. My husband speaks only French, vile you…" She looked at him questioningly.

"Only English," he supplied.

"I zought so." And then she exclaimed, gazing at the concrete tableau below, "But ze horreur! No citizens, zhust soldiers!"

"Where?"

"At ze gangplank, by ev'ry rope," she said, gutteralizing her r's in a delightfully feline way. "You haven't zeen? Over ze sides?"

"Not yet."

"Eh bien, it's not so much!" she declared, in careless Gallic fashion.

After their breakfast, he moved to the railing and looked down briefly. It was true. There was nothing but soldiers, each of them carrying automatic firearms. By then, the ship's loudspeakers were issuing directions for disembarkation in various languages. Jon hastened to his stateroom to collect the battered hat and a Leningrad map. Then he joined his fellow passengers, pushing toward the lower lobby and the gangway exit.

A young man Jon had not noted before bumped into him. "Sorry!" he said with a British accent. They edged downwards together for one flight but then were separated, as passengers from the lower deck shoved and insinuated themselves into the mainstream. By the time Jon reached the top of the gangplank, the young man was already at its foot.

Several soldiers stood checking visas prior to letting passengers touch Russian concrete. Once past the soldiers, the travelers entered a building attached to the concrete slab. Spacious, unencumbered by furnishings of any kind, the building's vastness emphasized its emptiness and so conveyed an air of magnificence unachieved—that is to say, of a project underfinanced and incomplete. There were multiple aisles and multiple gates, but only one of each seemed to be in service.

Beyond the building a dozen or so buses awaited the *Queen Anne's* passengers. Jon discovered and climbed aboard the single bus for English-speaking tourists. Because the vehicle filled to only about two-thirds, he had a seat and window to himself—a blessing, considering his size. He was heavy only in the sense of being a large man: tall, big-boned, broad-shouldered.

Waiting for the tour to begin, Jon saw the young British man enter and take the seat across the aisle. A resolve to make the young man's acquaintance was anticipated by the other, who asked, "You're American, aren't you?" Now his accent sounded not at all British.

Jon introduced himself.

"Wally Macleod," announced the other, extending his hand.

He looked about thirty and wore a Rolex watch in presumably 18 karat gold, Jon noted. "I don't recall seeing you before this morning."

"Right you are! I joined the cruise at Helsinki."

But further conversation had to be postponed because a Russian tourist guide dashed into the bus and immediately began her spiel—an error-filled presentation loosely based on the history of the German siege of Leningrad. She quickly produced incredulous stares from Jon and the rest of her relatively sophisticated audience—stares that would prove a recurrent feature throughout the day. She did not allow contentious questions about the long queues in front of stores, the Soviet military, or the secret service, nor did she brook corrections to her vocabulary. At one point she directed passengers to note the ornate German "watch" high atop a government building, and when a young American cheerily pointed out that the word was "clock," she looked at him as if he were one of several varieties of unsegmented worms. Another passenger asked why the clock was seven hours off, and she commented that the device was "of German design," which seemed explanation enough.

As the bus trundled over lumpy, pot-holed streets, Jon decided that the appurtenances on Soviet buses did not include springs. Passengers braced their feet and otherwise tensed ill-advisedly, while the bus passed along treeless avenues lined with blockish concrete apartment buildings, rusted construction machinery, untended lawns, and ugly red banners bearing Communist slogans. The guide described these abominations with enthusiasm except when she blamed them on the German or East-European architects who migrated to the country after the Second World War. Much of her commentary was given over to a tedious outline of the red tape and delays young couples experienced while waiting for acceptance at one of the 400-square-foot apartments filling the concrete boxes. Her presentation seemed designed to convince her audience that such impediments indicated an orderly, organized society.

"Now we come to the Neva," she announced, as they entered an area touched with the grace and elegance of former times. Despite the weeds in public gardens, the uncut parks, the cracked stonework, and the shutters hanging askew, the grand lines of the avenues and building facades spoke unmistakably of a more discriminating order, of an age when design and beauty were treasured. In short, the buildings and prospects eloquently testified to existence prior to the twentieth century.

"Now we will alight at the Museum of Atheism," their guide next advised, as the bus came to a halt before the gracefully colonnaded structure that in its day was thought to rival St. Peter's in Rome. She continued her spiel as passengers disembarked around her: "Begun in 1801 as Kazan Cathedral, it was later known as the Museum of the History of Religion and Atheism...."

The last to file from the bus, Jon paused to take in the scene once he reached the pavement. Then, preferring a walk around the deteriorating grounds to visiting the desecrated interior, he headed for the shade of the surviving trees.

Wally Macleod, either indecisive or waiting, had stood near the cathedral steps. Now he followed after Jon and soon fell in step, saying, "They say it's the hottest summer in a hundred years here. Everything looks dried up."

"Yes," returned Jon absently, for he was appraising the cathedral's foundations.

"So you're Jon Olsen! I met your cousins—well, whatever they are—in Helsinki. The Andersons."

"Oh?" inquired Jon, and he stopped walking, his attention wholly captured. "Second cousins," he advised, watching Macleod.

"They send their best," said Macleod, a little lamely. He evidently had expected Jon to say more.

"Where are they?"

"I'm not sure. They were called away suddenly."

"Not bad news, I hope." Jon looked at him intently.

"Oh, I suppose there's always a chance of that, when you're called away. You know, a war's going on or there's a death in the family or somebody's lifted your emeralds. On the other hand, you could be inheriting a fortune."

Macleod tried to look absolutely indifferent to the Andersons' real fate, but something about the subtle emphasis he placed on the last option made Jon suspect it was important and that Macleod knew more than he was saying.

During this exchange, they had resumed their leisurely pace. Jon was wearing his floppy hat, and he had glimpsed his reflection enough in shop windows to know that sometimes the hat and scar produced a semi-ridiculous result and at others a remotely sinister one. For some reason, he hoped the effect at this moment as they passed under the lofty trees was one that Macleod might view as intimidating.

Jon asked, "How did you meet Rudi and Xenia?"

"I visited their jewelry shop in Helsinki."

"Many people must come to their shop. That doesn't necessarily result in friendship."

Macleod laughed. "No, you're quite right. We got to talking. I'm very interested in jewelry, you see. And when I mentioned going to Leningrad on the *Queen Anne*—well, that's how your name came up."

"I see." But perhaps he did not see, for he peered at Macleod like a scientist studying a germ. He next asked, "So how are they, my second cousins?"

"Well, fine, I guess. Look, I was only in their shop. A totally casual encounter."

By now, the temperature and light exercise were causing Jon to perspire. He could feel dampness against the faille hatband at his temples and the silk shirt across his back. He thought how the day would grow hotter, how interiors would be stifling, how tempers would flare.

He stopped to wipe his brow with a cotton handkerchief and turned away from Macleod in the process. The younger man shoved his hands in his blazer pockets and walked a few paces off to examine one of the trees. In his light summer jacket, he seemed impervious to the sun.

However, as the day proceeded and the passengers moved from the Kazan to other former cathedrals, then through a lunch at which beer, champagne, and vodka flowed both liberally and simultaneously, the heat became such that even Macleod removed his coat. Moreover, the tour guide—clearly operating on the theory that people will believe what they are told regardless of what they otherwise perceive—announced twice that all St. Petersburg hotels were fully air-conditioned.

By the time the bus reached the Hermitage, everybody without exception perspired freely, so that those who had begun the day smartly dressed now seemed mussed and rumpled. They were all herded through a small side door where a disagreeable old hag collected tickets and cobwebs. Thence, after filing through an unprepossessing passageway, they were conducted into the sudden grandeur of the Winter Palace's glittering entry hall, marred only by an enormous number of visitors crowding the marble floors and staircase.

Jon's tour group was engulfed by the crowd and was swept relentlessly up the magnificent stairs. He looked all about him, but even with the advantages of the elevation and his height, he could not spot Macleod, nor did he see his countryman subsequently during the visit. Meanwhile the irresistible flow of humanity propelled Jon and his companions to the top of the staircase and into a large, gorgeous room, where the nightmarish crowd could not dwarf two huge malachite vases.

Jon began using his hat as a fan while they streamed slowly about the room. It was difficult to judge the treasures because of the horde, both native and foreign in composition. Perhaps because he intensely disliked being part of a mob, he had an uneasy perception that the storming of the Winter Palace was being restaged with himself as a participant.

Their guide had raised her arm straight up in the air as soon as they reached the top of the stairs, thus giving them a standard to follow. Now she swerved toward one of the several doorways and led them out, into an adjacent and only slightly less overrun room. Objects could be viewed there, albeit between the faces of strangers: Dutch school boys, Siberian bureaucrats, Austrian tradesmen, and Ukranian peasants.

They found themselves in a section devoted to religious art—an area of little interest to Jon. He nonetheless recognized Raphael and knew, because of his Grandfather Strasser's art dealings, how the Hermitage had once housed the celebrated *Alba Madonna* as well. The Tsars' art collection had once comprised all that one saw in the Hermitage today plus all that the Soviet government sold to Western capitalists to finance its First Five Year Plan and others.

Jon found himself thinking about those sales as he moved from gallery to gallery, from masterpiece to masterpiece. During the Soviet era there were the twin ironies of capitalist assistance to a Communist government and of Communist dependence on monarchial acquisitions. And there were more involuted subtleties, such as the status of works of art originally purchased by Russian Tsars from European princes and later confiscated by a revolutionary government.

Had the Bolsheviks sold national treasures, or had they sold stolen property? And if national treasures, how odd for any legitimate government to part with them voluntarily and how odd the painters were Dutch, Italians, French, and so on. But if they were stolen property, how strange the government returned none to rightful heirs, and how strange so many respectable people bought openly from a fence—even though the fence was a government entity.

Looking about him, Jon felt even more mystified by the fate of the unsold part of the collection. Here was the Hermitage, thronged not only by foreigners from whose countries many works had come, but also by Russian citizens, many of whom were automatons of the Communist state. They were sitting on Louis XV chairs in filthy work clothes—no matter if this dirtied and wore the upholstery bare. They were crossing themselves, Orthodox style, before figures of the Christ—no matter that Christianity was still frowned upon in contemporary Russia. They were opening drapes and windows the better to see and feel Rembrandts—no matter that this practice cracked the paint and allowed moisture, dust, and pollen to settle over them. Thus had the Bolsheviks—and before them, the French peasants—made their revolution.

And as he stood in the heat, among the crowd, looking at the Rembrandt peeling in the sunlight from an open window, Jon felt suddenly so oppressed he moved outside to put such neglect behind him. Yet his purpose was frustrated, because the paint on the railing outside was peeling, too. Impatiently, he turned from the sight and began making his way from the room. The crowds more than irritated him now, as he worked through and against them, from room to room, while retracing his route. He had a sense of being in the Tsars' palace, the Tsars' home, really; of himself and the others as intruders, even possibly thieves. He felt soiled, almost contaminated, by association with the mob, and he used his big shoulders and strong arms to good advantage in getting out of the Hermitage as fast as possible.

Back on the street, it was definitely the twentieth century. Scores of Hungarian-made tour buses occupied the square once dominated by mounted Cossacks and hussars. Where Imperial Eagles once flew, mundane Soviet banners now proclaimed mindless phrases.

He looked above his hands, under the brim of his hat, at the palace from which he had just escaped. There he saw Wally Macleod leaving by another door, obscure and removed from the entrance their party had used. He was shaking hands with a uniformed Soviet official. Jon leaped behind a bus before Macleod caught sight of him.

CHAPTER 4

▼

Carrying a purse and a piece of hand luggage, Violet Strasser stepped from the Scandinavian Airlines plane. As she did not expect her nephew Jon in Oslo until Saturday, there was no one to meet her flight. Accordingly she was amazed to hear her name repeated in a questioning way just after having her passport stamped. Looking beyond the barrier in the direction of the voice, she saw a willowy, blonde young woman.

"Ms. Strasser?" the young woman called again. "You are Violet Strasser?"

Violet passed to the other side of the barrier before answering, "Yes. Yes I am." By now she had found her baggage, which was moving along a conveyer belt.

The blonde, pushing an empty cart, meanwhile had reached the same place. She held out her hand. "I'm Anna Nygaard, from the Embassy. I'm the person who wrote to you. Let's just get your bags on this thing, and talk afterwards." Suiting action to words, Anna hoisted the bags onto the cart, carefully positioning the hand luggage on top.

Obligingly, Violet moved out of the way, while nonetheless proceeding to set matters straight. "I'm not 'Ms. Strasser,'" she advised without rancor. "I'm too old for contrived forms of address. You may call me Miss Strasser without offending my sensibilities at all." She smiled at the young woman. "Now if *you* prefer being addressed as 'Ms.,' I'm happy to do so."

"Excellent!" exclaimed Ms. Nygaard, and then immediately smiled back. Her smile was pleasant enough, thought Violet, but did not light up the world, perhaps because her natural beauty required no pyrotechnic aids for impact.

"You prefer 'Ms.'?" Violet inquired curiously.

"Anna's fine."

"That's settled then. Well, how very nice of you to meet me!"

As they walked through the airport, Anna pushed the cart. She also mentioned, in response to Violet's question, that Oslo was her first Foreign Service assignment—a most lucky draw, she said. "Usually you get Lagos or some such place on your first tour," she added brightly.

"What's Lagos?"

"The pits." Again she smiled.

They left the terminal building to find Anna's compact car, an orange Ford Fiesta, almost immediately in front of them in a no-parking zone. A nearby attendant smiled indulgently at Anna and even helped her with Violet's bags. The attendant was male.

Once the car began pulling away, Violet remarked, "I wonder if that young man's always so helpful."

"Diplomatic privilege."

"Oh! Do you meet every American arriving at Fornebu!"

"Certainly not."

"Then, why me?" asked Violet, assuming an air of innocence.

Her new acquaintance remained silent for a number of seconds. Then she shook her head, so causing her long, pale, silky hair to stir and realign itself in an almost simulated way, as if the product of years of cosmetic conditioning or trick photography. She eventually said, "We try to be of every help in these cases."

"What cases?"

"Well, deaths, you know."

"How thoughtful. But I haven't seen Yelena in sixty years or so. I suppose you already know things like that."

Anna did not answer, but asked a question instead. "So you're not affected?"

"Well, of course I'm affected when a person dies." In a moment Violet added, "She was the most beautiful woman I ever saw. Only bear in mind, that's a child's evaluation.

"Oh, she was beautiful all right. I've seen photos."

"At the end, do you mean?" inquired Violet, with the curiosity of one uninitiated to morgues.

"No. When she was young." Anna glanced at her passenger quickly. Returning her gaze to the road, she volunteered, "You may need our assistance. The Embassy's, I mean. You don't speak Norwegian, I suppose?"

Violet admitted she did not.

"Well, there'll be lawyers, officials. And problems, I should think. I'll brief you later, after you've settled in."

"Oh," exclaimed Violet, "you can brief me now. I'm wide awake!"

After another noticeable pause, Anna replied, "I'd rather not, while I'm driving."

Violet felt that Anna was neither inexperienced at driving nor at her job. Instead, she felt the girl was being evasive. Nevertheless, feeling mildly rebuked, she gave her full attention to the scenery—that is to say, to the city she had not visited for over thirty years. Of course, she had just implied to Anna that almost sixty years might have elapsed between visits. But no matter. Truth is not always served by scientific discoveries, much less by mere conversations.

The fact is, thirty years earlier Violet had become infatuated with a Norwegian named Tryggvi. She had rushed to Oslo, more or less at the would-be lover's invitation, and there occurred exquisitely excruciating days of unprofessed ardor and unrealized passion. The romance unresolved, she left town in the belief that all things remained possible, that love was there for the taking—if only she would.

The Countess of Dahlmark—a lifelong friend and one of Europe's legendary gossips—once told her, "Tryggvi did love you, Violet, more than any of the others. And that made him afraid, afraid the love would dissipate upon familiarity, the same as all the others." In short, Tryggvi seems to have been self-centered and somewhat immature.

Violet was exceptionally slow in realizing that the affair might gradually dissolve rather than be resolved. For at least five years following her Oslo visit, she lived for Tryggvi's communications, parsimonious as they invariably proved to be. Not a day came that she did not think of him; not a night, that she did not dream. Then one day she simply made an end of it, like a suicide or murder.

But now, in her sixties, returning to his city—no longer his—and passing along its streets—momentarily not the same streets—she discovered with some alarm that she could think fondly of him still. This unwelcome revelation caused her to move restlessly in her seat and to say abruptly, "The traffic's terrible! I don't wonder at your reluctance to discuss things! What's become of Oslo?"

"Oil," said her companion.

"I beg your pardon?"

"North Sea oil. It's made Norway rich, and Oslo big."

"It's made Oslo *noisy*!" sniffed Violet.

Yet despite this diversion, Tryggvi stayed very much on her mind and just as he looked so long ago: tall, Nordic, a bit bandy-legged. He had warmly blonde hair and icily blue eyes. He danced like a prince and smiled like a god. Recalling, Violet experienced a small shiver of appreciation, which vastly annoyed her.

Memories resemble ghosts more than anything else. They materialize at unexpected moments and spoil house parties. And here was Tryggvi's ghost threatening her equanimity, not to say her Oslo adventure.

As they passed the Radhuset, Violet exclaimed impatiently, "Surely we're about there!"

"A couple more blocks."

"I'm sorry if I sound testy!"

"You must be tired."

"No, I've seen something."

"Along the way? What?"

"A ghost of some sort," replied Violet, sounding detached.

"A ghost!" Anna's eyebrows shot up. "I'm not sure I can handle the supernatural!"

Violet felt Anna inspect her while they waited on a traffic light, but she merely raised her head high and studiously avoided the young woman's gaze.

Very shortly they arrived at Violet's hotel, with the predictable sequence of checking in and establishing occupancy. Anna accompanied her to the desk, but not to the room. They agreed to meet for tea in about twenty minutes to discuss Violet's situation.

During the interval Violet did such things as change her shoes from sensible to high-heeled ones and relocate her tickets from handbag to wardrobe case. She also extracted several documents from a compartment of her hand luggage and, after fitting on her reading glasses, scanned the English-language papers hurriedly. Next she pulled off the glasses and collapsed them with a snap, while eying herself in the mirror. She began pulling a recalcitrant strand of hair—dyed rich chestnut in honor of her lost youth.

She considered the oddity of being remembered in Yelena's will. Their relationship was tenuous, to say the least. They were related through the marriage of distant cousins, so there was no blood tie at all. And in their entire lives they met only twice: once in Violet's childhood and again in her thirties.

True, she had misled Anna Nygaard on that score. She honestly could not decide why she'd lied. Because she felt ashamed of the outcome with Tryggvi? Because of the inconclusive conversation with Yelena? Because she mistrusted Ms. Nygaard as a result of so many anti-U.S. government movies and television shows? A little of each, perhaps.

CHAPTER 5

▼

This was the *Queen Anne*'s second day in Copenhagen, and passengers were boarding buses early for various destinations. Jon, who had signed up for a trip to Helsingør, stood near the bus designated for English-speaking tourists. He was having a final look around prior to boarding, when Wally Macleod approached in the company of a most noticeable woman, quite unknown to Jon.

"Hi! I'd like you to meet Georgia Beech. She's joining us for the Hamlet thing."

Jon lifted his hat, then shook hands. He said, "A pleasure," and tried not to stare beyond the accepted limits, although definitely inclined that way. Ms. Beech, of some indefinite age between 25 and 40, simply overwhelmed the male thought process with animal magnetism and a generous bosom.

When she spoke, it was in the flat, down-home tones of West Texas. "Morning. Looks like we've got good weather for the tour."

"Yes. Yes, it does."

"I've never liked Hamlet much. Maybe seeing his home'll help."

Jon narrowed his eyes and nodded. He was trying not to be obvious, since she must know her effect on men. "His home's a castle," he said.

She laughed in an open, friendly way. "Not real comfortable, I would guess. Not by today's standards, anyway. We'll soon see." She turned to Macleod, so presenting the profile of her remarkable form for Jon's uninhibited gaze. "Wally, are we going to let this man sit with us?" she asked teasingly.

Thus Jon came to be across the aisle from Mrs. Calvin Beech of Scott County, Kentucky, who raised and trained horses and exuded the life force. He learned in rapid succession that her outing with Macleod was by prearrangement. Her invalid husband remained back in the States, and she traveled the continent with yet another party. All the while, Jon forwent the novelty of the Danish countryside for the stimulation of Mrs. Beech.

As they talked, he became somewhat less preoccupied with her figure, with her sensuality. She expressed herself so directly, she gazed at him so forthrightly from the sea green eyes with gold-red lashes, that he found himself no longer thinking exclusively of how she might look unclothed and sometimes of what a delightful person she seemed to be.

He asked, "And how did you get into training horses?"

"When Cal got injured."

"Just like that?"

"There was nothing else to do," she replied simply.

"And you've made a success of it, I judge."

"Has she ever!" exclaimed Macleod.

Jon watched him just a fraction of a second before rejoining, "Do you race horses, Wally? Is that how you two met?"

Macleod looked surprised, and Georgia intervened with a laugh. "We met at the Derby, but not 'cause Wally races horses."

"Why then?"

"Because he bets on them." Again the laugh. "You're very inquisitive!" she chided. "I reckon it's my turn to ask questions."

"By all means."

Her eyes widened. They had a distinctly luminescent quality, so much so that Jon wondered idly whether they glowed in the dark, like phosphorus, and whether the best test conditions might not be having her in bed.

She said, "All right. Are you traveling alone?"

"Well, yes. I didn't have the alternative of traveling with you." He folded his arms on the back of the seat in front and leaned a bit toward her.

"Why, thanks. I appreciate that, but it makes the next question harder."

"Why's that?"

"I was going to ask why you travel alone."

"It didn't occur to me to do otherwise, although now I realize the error of my ways."

She laughed lightly, with a little heave of her provocative chest, stored in a frivolous white blouse with a bateau neckline, worn above tapered black slacks. A bright cummerbund accented the demarcation between luxuriant superstructure and slender underpinnings. Her strawberry blonde hair fell gracefully in disobedient curls, and rings adorned every other finger.

Jon smiled and looked away, because she unnerved him. He felt he must get hold of himself, that the reserve of years was about to crumble. He had not built the reserve to have it fall apart so easily.

She was saying, "You must have some vice. I guess you beat your wife."

It got his attention. "My wife?"

"You probably beat the kids, too."

"You make it sound so matter-of-fact," he replied with a smile.

Macleod now joined the banter. "His kids 're all bastards."

"Really!" she exclaimed.

"I'm a bachelor," explained Jon, thinking the time had come.

She seemed not to hear and asked Macleod, "How many does he have?"

"Oh, dozens."

"In a variety of colors? Of countless nationalities?"

"Certainly."

She turned to Jon. "Can you name all of them?" And then she smiled so infectiously, so deliciously, that he had to look away again, pretending interest in the view outside the window. It was a long, long time since he had felt so stimulated.

He wondered if he truly liked the sensation. Wasn't it more satisfactory to take an academic stance towards one's own philanderings, thus keeping them contained? After all, she might be the stuff dreams are made of, but the dreams were strictly at the level of a shipboard romance, of the inconsequential lover—sensational for a week and faithful for roughly the same amount of time.

While arguing thus with himself, he caught only phrases from his companions' chatter: "…Lloyd's in London…" "…sometime tomorrow…" "…what Felix wants…" He joined in again when he could present his customarily unperturbed visage, deceptively enlivened by the scar marring his cheek; when, in short, he could be his apparent self.

Yet the seed of discontent had been planted, so that while the three discussed Shakespeare and castles in anticipation of their visit to Helsingør, a small part of him rebelled. A small part declared that a once-in-a-lifetime tour of Kronborg castle held little genuine significance, that discussions of Hamlet merely repeated opinions expressed often and for century upon century. A small part lamented an outing that brought him Georgia Beech only at arm's length.

Meanwhile, Macleod had taken their conversation quite seriously, for he now declared with heat, "It's pretty obvious you're both hostile to Hamlet!"

"I merely said he's neurotic," Jon defended himself.

"That's hostile!"

And Georgia said, "Face it, Wally. A fellow seeing ghosts has got systemic problems."

"You entirely disregard his time frame! People believed in ghosts then!"

"Well, sure," agreed Georgia, "if they were neurotics. That's the test for medieval neurotics: they see ghosts." And she began counting saints and sinners on her bejeweled fingers, while Macleod scowled so fiercely he looked like a medieval neurotic himself, and a Scottish one at that. He accused her at last, "You're making everything up! 'Babbalard' and 'Hellespont,' my ass!"

Jon laughed out loud, as Georgia tried to soothe the irate Macleod with apologetic admissions of her teasing, but to no effect. Macleod scorned their companionship after that. He turned his face from them and displayed as much of his back as he could while staring grimly out the window—a pose that persisted the remaining way to Helsingør.

When the bus unloaded, Georgia preceded Macleod, who went before Jon. Jon's upbringing would never permit him to barge ahead of a person with greater rights to a lady, regardless of the strength of any longings to do so. To his immeasurable relief, Macleod huffed off the moment he hit the pavement, so leaving Georgia to the wolves. Certainly, Jon fancied the role.

With the speed of a pounce, he took her by the arm and guided her toward the bridge leading to Kronborg castle. Gazing down at her shining ringlets and bateau neckline, he felt absolutely transported. Suddenly the slightly overcast day was the brightest in years.

She looked up and asked, "Why are you smiling?"

He wanted to answer, "Because I love you, Mrs. Beech!" Instead, maintaining an outwardly cool and expressionless face, he said, not entirely untruthfully, "Because Wally's gone."

"You don't like him?"

"I want you to myself."

"Thanks, I like you, too. But Wally invited me."

"Well, but he's left you to me, it seems. I certainly like him for that."

"You don't really like him," she decided.

"He's…bad tempered."

"That's unfair. We provoked him."

"'We'?"

"It was *you* who laughed," she reminded him.

They had reached the bridge and now started across. Above and to the right loomed the fortress that was Kronborg. Below flowed the channel dividing castle from town. On the bridge, as on the roads leading to and from it, walked tourists, including many from the *Queen Anne.*

Only now did Jon recognize, in the forms of people ahead, various Italian and Spanish passengers from the ship. This identification came as a shock to him, since, in his preoccupation with securing Georgia as his companion, he had entirely overlooked the presence of other buses where theirs had parked.

His failure was the more disturbing in that he normally displayed a keen power of observation. Even as a child he had shown proof of this trait, much to the joy of his father who hoped Jon would follow in his footsteps in the timber industry. That an entire fleet of buses had just eluded him seemed almost sinister. Suppose his perceptions of Georgia were equally skewed!

"Hey!" exclaimed that lady, breathlessly, dragging a bit behind him. "Could you slow down? I can hardly keep up!"

He halted in his tracks, and she swung to a stop beside him. "I'm so sorry," he apologized, letting go of her arm.

She took a couple of deep breaths—a very interesting process, actually—and then smiled at him. "Okay. I'm revived." As she spoke, she touched his arm, and this act somehow ended very naturally in their holding hands while climbing the rest of the way to the fortress.

He dedicated himself to going slowly. In those few final minutes of passage, they, the sky, the sea, and the stonework seemed in total harmony. Such contentment, such peace pervaded the modest event of being together that Jon hallucinated eternity or some other perfection.

Unfortunately, it is the nature of perfection to be followed by imperfection. Reaching the portal, Georgia and he were obliged to proceed single file up a circular stone staircase, and although this arrangement had its compensations, it effectively ended the holding of hands. Moments later they arrived in a large, rectangular area, where visitors were separated like daffodils and clumped into tour groups.

In the new ambiance of crowds and commotion and interior gloom, eternity signified something closer to hell than heaven. There was an immediate, perceptible decline in civilized behavior, celebrated by several unruly Spanish children from the *Queen Anne* who chased one another through doorways and around their elders' legs.

While the groups were led in packs about castle and courtyard, Jon felt little inclination to claim Georgia's hand. On the contrary, his nature prompted a withdrawal from others, a hanging back from the pack. Evidently missing him, Georgia looked around. She waved when she spotted him, but neither moved toward the other. He continued to trail the group.

From this vantage point, he observed how Wally Macleod sidled up to Georgia, a smug smile on his face—or so Jon judged it. The fact was, during their few days' acquaintance, he had grown wary of Macleod, nor did his dislike stem entirely from that young man's ability to walk sweatless through museums un-air conditioned at 90 degrees Fahrenheit. No, nor was it jealousy even now, when Jon acknowledged Macleod's prior right to the company of the delectable Georgia Beech.

Rather, dislike grew from distrust—not the mild distrust one has for computer printouts, but the profound unease engendered by an armed man. Jon's wariness built gradually, from the time Macleod disappeared in Leningrad and reappeared with a Russian official. Wally subsequently had made a fairly obvious attempt at "cultivating" Jon, who possessed sufficient modesty to identify the effort, particularly since their conversations revealed a political and ethical divergence.

Of course, being younger, Wally may still have felt enthusiasm for most causes instead of satisfaction about a few things. Nevertheless, he was thirty at least and so presumably had constructed a fixed hierarchy of values for himself. That order apparently revolved around self-interest to the extent that the universe served in a satellite capacity.

Perhaps like others who lack both, Wally equated size and brawn with slowness and stupidity, in which case he may have hoped to manipulate Jon for some secret end. There was that side to Jon, of course: a stoic, immovable, imperturbable part that passed for his entire self. He knew it was easy to infer—mistakenly—a glacier like motion of mind and body in one so large, so laissez-faire, so independent.

Only Jon understood himself as a self-monitored volcano, possibly extinct, possibly merely dormant; as a person sufficiently refined to recognize his own vulgarity; as a man whose singleness was beginning to verge on loneliness. He understood himself and embraced that insight, as now, when he deliberately distanced himself from Georgia Beech. He did not care to risk the memory of so pleasurable a meeting by prolonging it on the chance of satisfying his lust. For the commonness underlying lust and romantic sentiment alike was that any two people could do it. Absolutely anyone.

It was too risky. He liked her too much. Either she would refuse him, so causing frustration, or accept him, so leading to infatuation. And when did infatuation ever result in anything other than boredom or betrayal? Besides, whatever game it was that Wally Macleod played, Georgia may have been assigned a part. First he joins the tour in Leningrad, then she hooks up in Copenhagen. Truly, something could be rotten in Denmark.

So he dawdled behind the rest of the pack at Helsingør. On they toured, with the cold, Northern light shafting through tall, slim windows. Twentieth century Spanish whelps yelped and scudded about the enormous banquet hall, unseen by Hamlet. The sea and Sweden, glimpsed across the narrow neck of the Oresund, looked little different from a hundred, a thousand years before. Within the memory of man, Jon mused, any afternoon is much like any other, except when cannon roar or earthquakes strike.

CHAPTER 6

▼

One of the good things about this Baltic-Sea cruise, Jon would later tell Aunt Violet, was the way arrival times were arranged so that the *Queen Anne* pulled into port during daylight hours—usually in the morning—thus allowing tourists ample time to arrange and participate in tours of the cities at which the ship docked. None of this arriving in port at dusk or later and being forced to spend the night on board while the lights of Helsinki or Copenhagen or Oslo beckoned and tantalized over the shimmering water separating city and ship.

And so he enjoyed the *Queen Anne*'s leisurely arrival at the port of Oslo, the city at first an uneven bump on the distant horizon, then a crenellated grouping of buildings seen hazily, and finally a great metropolis marked by bustling people and noisy vehicles. As the ship maneuvered ever closer to the dock, nudged by two hard-working tugs, Jon spotted his Aunt, swathed in a dark silk dress and outdated hat with a bright orange mum dancing in the breeze. Beside her, hatless in a white linen frock, stood a tall, willowy blonde. As best he could tell from this distance, his aunt was conversing with the woman.

Jon searched the ship's crowd to say goodbye to Madame Perpignan, but her back was his final view as she struggled down the gangplank amidst—through some terrible miscalculation—a veritable wave of noisy teens and children. He could almost hear her mutters of "horreur" as she fought her way to the tour bus. As he glanced at the crowd, he sighed for the lovely Georgia Beech, but she, of course, was not among the throng oozing onto the gangplank, having continued on her way following their too-brief encounter in Denmark. He thought for a moment he spotted Wally Macleod, in a blue tam-o-shanter, leaning against the railing at the top of a stairway, but after picking up his bags and looking at the spot again, the figure had disappeared.

Jon made his way through Norwegian customs and thence into the arms of his aunt, who seemed more pleased than was her want to see him. They held each other for a moment, and Jon was struck with the realization that his Aunt, while still mentally as spry as a philosopher, was growing old and frail. Her eyes were clear and sparkling, but the bones of her shoulders and back stuck through the thin dress poignantly. He vowed to be more patient with her than in the past, rolling with her acerbic comments rather than responding to them.

After several utterances of joy, Violet broke away and gestured toward Anna. "Jon, I would like you to meet Anna Nygaard. She works for the American Embassy here and has been ever so helpful to me." She looked at the girl pointedly. "Isn't that right, Anna?"

"We try our best, M'am." Anna smiled, holding her hand out to Jon.

"How do you do?" he said, wondering why she was in Violet's tow if she was nothing more than a functionary of the embassy. Didn't she have more important duties?

"My, you're a tall one, aren't you," Anna said, looking him up and down. "I don't usually find myself gazing up at anyone, but you're a long drink of water, as they say in the States."

Jon wondered what part of the States she was referring to, but had to admit that, indeed, she likely didn't look up very often, calculating that she was close to six feet tall. "How long have you been posted to Oslo, Ms. Nygaard?"

"Please call me 'Anna.' Only stuffy old bureaucrats call me 'Ms. Nygaard—and I can tell you're not stuffy at all."

The day was breezy, and the young woman had a way of flicking her lustrous hair back into position with a wave of the head that Jon found almost unnerving. He wondered why he was noticing her physical attributes, feeling as he did about the gorgeous Mrs. Beech.

"You were on the verge of telling me about your posting?" He picked up his bags and began walking toward a parking lot he assumed had a car that would take them away from the docks. They followed in his wake.

"Oh, that," she said, dismissively. "Since Miss Strasser and I have discussed it at some length, I didn't want to bore her by repeating everything. Suffice to say, I've been here a few years—more than one and fewer than ten."

"How do you like it?"

"The winters are too long and the summers too short. Other than that, I find it tolerable." Jon had turned to look at her during this recitation, and she took that moment to again flick her golden locks into perfect alignment. "Oslo's not Washington D.C., but there are far worse assignments."

"Oh, you're from D.C.?"

Aunt Violet, perhaps feeling left out of the conversation, broke in, "She's from Milwaukee—comes from a long line of Wisconsin Swedes—but she went to school in Washington."

"Exactly," Anna said. "I attended Georgetown for a while. That's where the State Department recruited me. I speak all the Scandinavian languages, which explains why I'm here, I suppose. It's a case of one's background coming back to haunt her."

And so the conversation went, sometimes flowing, sometimes fitful, while Anna drove them through Oslo with nimble expertise, to finally arrive at Violet's hotel where a room had been reserved for Jon. After cleaning up and donning fresh clothing, he joined them in the hotel restaurant, where they had found a table in a walled courtyard with mature birch trees and tall, stately Douglas firs blocking most of the noonday sun.

Jon trusted Anna to order one of the local dishes for him, while he perused the wine list and ordered a bottle to be shared by all. He drank rather more than usual, faster than he normally did, and before long he was feeling languid and not a little tipsy as the glasses and bottles began to add up. He heard snippets of a long discussion about the role of Scandinavian peoples in the American Midwest and the loss of their cultures in the great melting pot of America—little of which interested him, in spite of his own Swedish background. He wondered why nobody broached the topic of why they were gathered there, in Oslo. The scene reminded him of a recent movie, set at the turn-of-the-century, featuring a well-dressed man, beautiful young woman, and dowager aunt, sitting in a hotel courtyard, with dappling sunlight, vintage wine, and hazy premonitions all about. What *was* it called?

After completing her lunch—with, Jon noted, two glasses of wine, something of a rarity for her—Violet excused herself, saying she was tired from her travels and needed a nap. As she got up to leave, she looked pointedly at the empty wine bottles and the two young people, and Jon was sure he saw something like disapproval in her eyes. "I'm having dinner with Rudi and Xenia this evening, so you will have to take care of yourself. Will you be alright?" And after several assurances she took her leave.

Following her departure, Jon and Anna continued to drink and converse, the topics switching rapidly, as topics will when the participants are newly acquainted and approaching intoxication. At some point Anna changed from wine to beer. Jon worried that she would become ill, given the amount of wine she had drunk, but he could not dissuade her from it. Later—he could not be sure how much later—a waiter stumbled on a cobblestone in the courtyard and spilled wine on Anna's white linen dress. After fending off the waiter's lamentations, Jon suggested they wash it with a detergent he always brought on trips, and she agreed, averring that it was her favorite summer frock and she feared the stain would set permanently if she did not tend to it quickly.

Somehow, they made it to Jon's room—he could not be sure he paid the bill before leaving the restaurant—where she blotted the dress with his detergent and a washcloth. The conversation continued unabated, which required shouted responses between the bathroom and bedroom. He sat on the only chair in the room, while sipping the glass of wine he had brought from downstairs, and was soon joined by Anna, who had managed to remove the stains entirely from her dress.

"Communism is one of the real bummers of our times," Anna was saying, plopping on the edge of the bed, a stein of Norwegian beer still in her hand. "Peter the Great may have been an elitist pig who ruled over a starving nation, but at least he discriminated between a beheading and the totally banal." As she said this, she sat cross-legged near the edge of the bed, her full skirt tucked prudently.

Jon wondered how they made it out of the restaurant with a glass of wine and stein of beer. Had he paid for them? Perhaps he gave his room number and they charged everything to it. Looking around, he could hardly believe his companion and surroundings, much less the conversation. How was it that Aunt Violet had disappeared, leaving him in a Norwegian hotel room with one of the world's great junior beauties? Because he honestly couldn't remember the exact sequence of events leading up to this situation, he judged himself tolerably well drunk.

"I mean," Anna was going on, looking at him earnestly with large, sparkling, thickly fringed eyes, "they sandwich an execution between deodorant ads and soccer scores. That way nothing's serious, everything's insipid."

He looked down into his own drink and confined his response to an ambiguous monosyllable.

"You agree?"

He heard himself say, "Peter was great."

"No. I mean about our times."

"All times are summations."

She leaned closer, quite close, peering curiously into his face. "What an interesting thought! Are you a Marxist?"

"No. No, of course not!"

"Well, it was an interesting thought. Awesome, in fact! Only I can't quite make you out. You look like a pirate, but you dress like a banker. Except now, of course, you've got your sleeves rolled up."

He glanced at his bare forearms. "When did I do that?"

"I don't know exactly. Before we came here. But you look like a pirate," she repeated.

"My sleeves are rolled up."

"Are you drunk, Jon?" she asked with sudden inspiration. Then she went right on, "I can't tell at all what you think. You don't seem to have a definable facial expression. Isn't that odd? I mean, most people have facial expressions."

He noticed he was sitting backwards on a straight chair, his arms propped across the top. It seemed to him the chair was rather small, but then, most chairs were,

"Of course," she said, scrutinizing him, "It's the scar that makes you look like a pirate. Bankers don't have scars. They have plastic surgery." She reached across to trace his scar with her finger. "God, it's real!"

Quite without thinking he caught her hand, because touching him like that invaded his personal space.

She exclaimed, "You're lovely, Jon!"

Realizing he had hold of her hand, he released her in panic.

"It's such a wonderful scar! How did you get it?"

"It was free."

"How did it happen?" she persisted.

"A bayonet."

"Goodness! You're lucky to be alive!"

For an instant, the entire scene—inexorable rain, gray jungle, bloody foxhole—flashed through his mind, and he felt less disembodied. "Yes, I'm lucky," he agreed.

"The thing is," she said, taking up her stein in both hands again, "You can't be a pirate if your scar's from a bayonet. At least, it's unlikely. So that changes our relationship."

"Why?"

"Well, you're somebody else," she explained, taking a drink.

He made an effort to salvage reality. "I'm always the same."

"That's your outward image."

"I'm always the same," he insisted.

"I simply can't relate to that."

He was having a little difficulty relating, himself. Here he was, somehow separated from everyone—Aunt Violet, Rudi, Xenia—except this lovely nymphet. What was she doing in his room? He supposed he must have invited her.

"I mean, everything changes," she said, only slightly slurring her words. "Think of the universe, starting out the size of a pea! Or you, starting the size of a sperm! Everything changes, Jon," she told him solemnly, setting her beer aside to lean forward once more, hands on her knees.

He had the sensation of being a sophomore again and didn't like it, especially since no girl in his sophomore class would have dreamed of mentioning sperm. He made another valiant attempt at rationality. "What do you think of Rudi?"

"Who?"

"Rudi Anderson."

"Is he the one who sings 'Love Me Among the Paper Lanterns?'"

Given this clue that she, too, was well drunk, he remained silent. He was envisioning the grim necessity of seeing her home—wherever that was—and of rediscovering his hotel sometime before dawn. Drunk as he was, that might not be an achievable goal.

"Jon, love," she now said, taking him by the shoulders so that their faces were dangerously close, "if you're not a pirate, who are you?" She kissed his forehead, then his scar.

"Anna…"

"Who are you?" She was kissing along the scar, to the edge of his lips, then kissing his lips. "Who?"

He kissed back, of course. At this point there was no possibility of good judgment. The kiss lasted about a minute, during which they both came to their feet and he kicked away the chair.

"Jon," she murmured, running her long fingers through his hair.

She was fully six feet tall, and the top of her head came to about his chin. Pressing her face to his shoulder, he surveyed the bed. Now he remembered his impression of the room that morning: it was very small. A small room with a short bed. A room designed for gnomes.

"Do you love me?" she asked, raising her head. Before he could kiss her again, she suddenly disappeared from view, and an unexpected weight filled his arms. Anna had passed out.

He laid her across the bed—diagonally, so her feet could be supported. When he had straightened up, he ran a hand over his face, as if to refresh himself. The need for decision had penetrated his comfortable, alcoholic haze.

Nevertheless he stood there looking at tall Anna on the short bed. She was very beautiful and, by his measure, quite young. She had ash blonde hair, and the juxtaposition of highlights and shadow reminded him of snow leopards. Her slenderness evoked willows or birch. Not even his height seemed adequately to explain such a creature finding him attractive so quickly.

He decided to shower, as an antidote to both drunkenness and the heat. Afterwards there would be the question of where to sleep, but he would wisely deal with such decisions one thing at a time. Accordingly, he stripped, showered, and toweled off in a matter of minutes.

Then he stood in the buff, which was his customary nightwear. Immediately the next problem confronted him: what to wear to bed when one had visitors and no pajamas. Electing for tennis shorts, he wrapped himself in the bath towel and went into the adjoining room.

Anna lay exactly as he had left her. He looked for his suitcase, found it, and hoisted it to the rack provided. Discovering he couldn't open it without a key, he searched for his discarded trousers. Meanwhile, every time the towel slipped, he clutched it back around him.

At last unlocking the suitcase, he found the shorts, put them on, and tossed away the towel. These actions left him facing the ultimate question: where to sleep? Anna occupied the meager bed, the chairs were too small, and the shower came in a stall rather than over a tub. That seemed to leave only the floor as a possibility.

He looked at the floor, covered with a dark, commercial-grade carpet. Visually it appeared clean, although germs doubtless incubated on every strand. More to the point, the room was very small and heavily furnished, so there was no six-and-half feet of clear space anywhere. Either his head must rest under the table or his feet, under the bed.

He located a spare blanket in a drawer. Taking a seat cushion from the one upholstered chair, he installed it under the table and carefully spread the blanket along the expected course of his body. Finally, he lay down.

By now the pleasant, alcoholic haze had lifted, and his mind revived. Bits and pieces of the day's events flashed into his consciousness along with flotsam and jetsam more remote in origin, such as the sound a bayonet makes against bone and the luminescence of Georgia Beech's sea green eyes.

For some reason he recalled Anna's driving tour of Oslo earlier in the day, including a brief stop at the Franklin Delano Roosevelt Memorial. The memorial looked strangely unkempt, and when Anna explained that drug deals were done there, he felt more than disappointment. Now, in the darkness, lying on the floor under a table, he again experienced the same sharp pang of perceived decay as under the memorial, except that the dark spawned its own breed of fantastical maggots. It was a decay, not of the memorial, not of youth—and neither of these decays alarmed, because both were inevitable—but of the very rocks, the Oslo fjord, of Nature herself.

He jerked fully awake from the abyss of sleep and rose abruptly on his elbows, so narrowly escaping a blow to the head from the solid birch tabletop above. After a moment, he laid back, and Nature quickly returned, no longer in obvious decay, but ghostly, amorphous. She swirled down from the Akershus fortress like wind-driven snow. She undulated along the docks of Oslo like Salome's seven veils, gently inducing sleep.

*   *   *   *

When Jon awoke, light streamed through the window whose drapes he had neglected to close. Despite momentary disorientation, he again avoided hitting the tabletop as he sat up to view the bed. Anna perched on its edge, her head in her hands.

"Good morning," he said.

She raised her eyes long enough to glare at him in martyred fashion. "It's the most ghastly morning I've ever seen!"

One look and he could see she considered the wages of sin a fate worse than death. "Maybe some fresh air would help—a nice walk in the park?"

"I just want to die."

"But afterwards, you'd be sorry." He found his socks and began putting them on, then his shoes. He stood near the bed, debating what to do next.

She looked at him and a wan smile broke through the frown. "You know, Jon, tennis shorts and black socks are not exactly *haute couture*—even in Oslo."

"I'll be glad to change into some more suitable combination. If I can find one in this mouse warren they call a room."

"How can you?"

"How can I what?"

"Move." She groaned. "After all we drank, how can you even stand, never mind walk about?"

"I'm bigger. It takes more drinks to put me under."

"That doesn't explain the near-death experience I'm having."

"The best thing to do," he advised, "is to become active. The sooner you move around, the sooner you'll feel better."

"Yes, yes!" she rather gasped, turning her face toward the wall.

Taking his own advice, he picked up a clean shirt and yesterday's trousers and withdrew into the bathroom. Upon showering and completing the desired transformation, he reopened the door, which happened to be located immediately next to the bed on the side where Anna suffered. By now she had fallen sideways and was kneading at the covers.

"Come on! Get up!" he urged, raising her to her feet.

She doubled over. "My head…it's ghastly!"

"Moving'll make it dissipate faster," he told her. "Come along!" And although there was going to be a certain hardship in navigating around the smallish room, crammed with furniture, he managed to drag her a few feet.

She moaned then exclaimed, "This can't be a cure!"

"It is," he said.

"It's persecution!"

"Why would I persecute you?"

"Why did Nazis persecute Jews?"

"Keep moving."

"I'm sick, Jon!" She planted her feet while arching her back in a cat-like defiance.

Of course, he could have forced her forward, but such a measure seemed impolite. "Very well," he conceded, "but you'll have to stay in bed for hours."

"Yes, yes!" she cried eagerly.

"Here, I suppose."

"Oh, I can't go anywhere!"

He looked at his watch. "I have to leave. I'll put out the sign, so they won't disturb you," and he began collecting his things: handkerchief, wallet, jacket.

"Where're you going?" she asked, again reclining on the bed.

"To Yelena's, remember? Rudi and Aunt Violet are cataloguing."

"They're looking for Imperial Eggs."

When he looked at her questioningly, she added, "Your aunt likes to talk."

"The Eggs are only part of it."

She squinted at as he shrugged into his jacket and deposited his wallet in the inside pocket.

"You must despise women!"

He couldn't control the look of surprise her words elicited. "Why would you say that?"

"A facial expression! Jon, how marvelous!"

"Of course I don't despise women," he replied, ignoring her second remark and carefully composing his face again. He picked up his passport and placed it with the wallet, then started for the door.

"Jon?"

He stopped and faced her. "Yes?"

"You mustn't think this happens every Saturday night!"

"I don't. It was bad wine."

"When I'm feeling better, I'll show you what a dignified, competent woman I can be."

"By all means."

He turned his back again, trying to hide a smile as he attached the "Do not disturb" sign to the doorknob. Then he closed the door softly and departed.

CHAPTER 7

▼

Rudi Anderson took no pride in the fact his wife was born a Russian, just as he did not congratulate himself on having married a woman twenty years younger. Far from pride and self-congratulation, he felt something akin to embarrassment. Himself more German than Swedish or Finnish, he had a certain obsession with detail, a certain passion for order that many consider Germanic traits. His wife Xenia conspicuously lacked both characteristics.

Born at the end of World War I, Rudi met his future wife in the wake of World War II. She had been about ten years old at the time, and he scarcely noticed her. Ten years later, they were married. It was his first marriage.

By then, Rudi was forty. He had established a good but limited reputation as a designer and fashioner of jewelry. Operating out of Helsinki, he was known—but not too well—to fellow artists and craftsmen in various cities abroad: Berlin, Stockholm, Oslo, even Paris. This reputation neither grew nor diminished by much in following years. A few Americans learned of his existence, but he never became a national or international fad.

It was in Paris that his romance with Xenia developed. Possibly for that reason, he seldom returned to Paris now. On the other hand,

Xenia had many relatives there whom she frequently visited. Perhaps Rudi avoided the relatives.

The couple lived comfortably in their Helsinki apartment house. Both worked in their jewelry shop, where Rudi kept the books in addition to creating jewelry. Xenia placed orders and handled sales, at which she did quite well, thanks to good taste and a real knack for discerning potential buyers' psychological weaknesses. Many people left their shop with items they had no inkling they desired prior to entering.

Thus businesswise, they made a good team, and in the matter of humdrum daily living as well. Xenia cooked and tended plants in those hours outside the shop, while Rudi drew his designs and plotted raw material acquisitions. Even housecleaning—so disinteresting a task for Xenia—was performed by a girl who came irregularly.

Rudi learned that his young bride's childhood had been difficult, born as she was in the Soviet Union just before the war. Without recalling the facts very precisely, she had seen military service and explosions and even battlefields. She had been cold and hungry and certainly very tired. Her family found itself among the vast numbers of homeless people, of displaced persons and active refugees. Unlike many Russian refugees of that period, her family escaped the awful fate of repatriation to Siberia or, worse, the gulags.

Despite disenchantment with the Soviet Union, Xenia's family remained unwaveringly pro-Russian. It was this more than any other attitude that made Rudi hostile towards his in-laws. Although only one-fourth Finnish, he thought as a Finn when he dealt with Russians. Russians were the enemy by any other name, be it Muscovy or the Soviet Union. Marriage with the enemy did not dispel old scores, as in a fairy tale, but merely curbed their outward expression.

Because Xenia and he did not really talk about matters other than their household and business, the marriage subsisted. Each knew almost nothing of what the other believed, of what lay in the heart. But not a detail of everyday behavior remained in any way obscure. Rudi knew precisely how Xenia applied her numerous cosmetics and could safely predict that she would wear high heels to climb stairs or a mountain. Xenia knew exactly how Rudi liked his coffee and what colors he could abide in socks. There were no surprises possible in such a marriage.

When Rudi decided to go to Oslo and so miss their cousin Jon's visit, he merely advised Xenia of the fact and gave her the choice of coming along or not. Xenia, on her part, simply announced she would accompany him without offering any reasons for electing to do so. They packed their things, loaded their Volvo, and embarked on the ferry without either ever referring to Yelena Anderson and their impending inheritance.

Among their luggage were several jeweler's cases. Wherever Rudi traveled, this type of case accompanied him to hold both his creations and his buys. Xenia and he could not live on the pleasant level they did, were they to depend on selling his works alone. They bought from numerous artisans and dealers at home and abroad for resale in their shop. He also picked up gems and metals on his trips. The absence of customs officers along certain routes facilitated such trade.

After ferrying to Stockholm and spending the night there, they drove on to Oslo, where, by Rudi's prearrangement, they took a room and bath in a private home known to him from prior visits. No sooner had they settled, than Rudi went off somewhere, and Xenia, too. Neither volunteered a destination nor asked what the other intended. They established what they considered the only needful information, namely, a time and place for meeting again.

Wherever else Rudi went, he at one point visited the Finnish embassy, for, like Violet Strasser, he had been named in Yelena Anderson's will. Unlike Violet, he was a blood relation to Ingmar Anderson, Yelena's late husband. Rudi's father and Ingmar were first cousins. As for Rudi's connection with the Strassers, it came through his mother, who was Violet's first cousin.

Rudi recalled very little about Cousin Ingmar, who died in 1933. For some reason, Cousin Ingmar had been in Switzerland at the time. Rather than transport the body back to Oslo—which, after all, Cousin Ingmar had merely adopted as home—Yelena arranged for his interment in Lausanne. Rudi's father journeyed to Switzerland for the services and passed both ways through Germany, which had recently acquired an Austrian-born chancellor named Adolf Hitler.

When Rudi's father returned to Helsinki, he remarked on the widow Yelena's great beauty and speculated that she quickly would marry again. His prediction of course proved quite wrong, for she went to her grave fifty years later still the widow of Ingmar Anderson. Many in the family considered such steadfastness to the memory of a dead husband noteworthy but odd.

Naturally Rudi knew Cousin Ingmar's history: how he went to St. Petersburg and worked for the house of Faberge, subsequently to become involved in various banking and financial matters; how the Russian Revolution turned Cousin Ingmar's world upside down and sent him home to Finland, where he joined General Mannerheim's White Army in its successful war against the Reds; how he brought Yelena with him and established her in Christiania while still himself fighting with Mannerheim in Finland.

All these events were mere history to Rudi, not quite born by then. However, he had ample occasion as an adolescent to observe Yelena while she yet possessed her fabled beauty. Later the Second World War intervened, and Rudi in his turn went to fight the Russians for Finland and Mannerheim. His remaining youth and half of middle age passed before he saw Yelena again. At sixty or so she was still beautiful, but age had rubbed out her once unsurpassed allure.

Rudi had no difficulties with Yelena's Russian-ness. For one thing, like so many Faberge work masters, Yelena's father was Finnish, making Yelena herself at least half Finnish and therefore more so than Rudi. For another, she belonged to that vanished European world of multilingual aristocrats, unapologetic elitism, and unshared wealth that alone allowed the execution of such exquisite ornaments as Faberge's. As a designer of taste himself, Rudi appreciated that world—the more so for the impossibility of taking advantage of it.

Yelena came once to his shop in Helsinki and asked to see his workbench. As she turned over the tools and examined Rudi's designs, she briefly reminisced, telling him about the layout of her father's shop in St. Petersburg and of the jewelry designers there. "It was always a matter of Carl Faberge's taste," she said, "whether an object proved acceptable. It was never anyone else's taste, least of all the unenlightened masses'. There were no plastic crosses in those days—Mr. Faberge would have been outraged."

There were no plastic crosses in Rudi's shop, either, but he knew what she meant: in the entire world of Faberge's time, no plastic existed or would have been tolerated. And also no electric guitars, no "designer" blue jeans, no massive portraits of Lenin or Stalin. She meant that the real tragedy of that world's end was its replacement by banality and the triumph of vulgarity. She meant that the blessings of mass production, mass communication, and medical advancement did not make up for the curse upon them.

Rudi refused to accept that view in its entirety. He believed no sensitive person living in his time could accept it and keep going. An atheist, he felt that without hope in a future life, one needed hope in this one. One had to subscribe to progress, to upward progress, even to future progress. One had to feel that if the sun collapsed tomorrow, it would produce a better world than the world destroyed. One had to.

Besides, he could compare his existence today with that during World War II and could honestly say things were better. Today he didn't stand sentry in freezing rain, nor march half-frozen across Karelian snow. He could listen to static-free tapes featuring the greatest symphony orchestras in the world, rather than mush through inclement weather to some second-rate local performance where people coughed incessantly. Moreover, he probably owed the continuance of his very life to the discovery of penicillin and antibiotics.

Nevertheless, he apprehended what Yelena meant and in part perceived what she perceived: that for her, the quality of life had declined. How much of that decline could be attributed to losing her husband, how much to simple aging, how much to civilization's fracturing, how much to life's new vulgarity, Rudi obviously couldn't say. But he understood sufficiently to feel a vague melancholy.

Now, at age sixty-four, he discovered himself her heir—together with Cousin Violet, of course. And whereas he did not exactly resent his American cousin's inclusion, he questioned it. The Americans had everything, everything modern, everything essential, every comfort. They did not need the graceful fancies of a bygone time.

Besides, there was his plan.

Rudi knew the greed of mankind to be boundless. Did he not count on it in his work? Did not Xenia play upon it in selling his wares so cleverly? And had not Mr. Wallace Macleod fallen victim to it in making his offer? Greed always came at a high price, and in this particular round, Rudi expected to name that price.

CHAPTER 8

▼

Like Jon, Wally Macleod left the cruise at Oslo. After the tour buses had departed, he descended the gangplank, a suitcase in each hand. A sailor from the *Queen Anne* held a cab for him and helped him stow his gear in the back seat.

Wally proceeded to a centrally located hotel, where he registered. There was a brief misunderstanding with the desk clerk, who tried to place him in the hotel's finest suite. He explained that the suite was not for him but for another member of Felix Ratliff's party—for Mr. Ratliff himself, no doubt—and finally got the matter straightened out. It occurred to Wally that someday the suite might be his rather than Ratliff's, but that would never be the case as long as he was the employee and Ratliff the employer. Of course, Ratliff also had an employer to whom he was answerable—the Soviet government itself—but that rarified relationship was so far removed from Wally's current position that it did not merit consideration. Not yet, anyway.

Once in his room, he removed his blazer, loosened his tie and snapped on the TV set. A most curious entertainer blipped onto the screen: a male singer, dressed like a troglodyte and evidently tone deaf, at whom an unseen audience hissed and jeered raucously. After a momentary stare of disbelief, Wally turned his attention from the Norwegian troll to one of his suitcases. After a short search, he fetched forth a spiral notebook.

Oblivious to the TV program, he sat, then lay on the bed while looking over entries in the notebook. There were columns of dates, letters—some single, some in groups—and finally notations, closely and often doubly packed on a given line. The notations typically read: "A rosebud, legend damaged/destroyed, photo only" or "M St. George cross, Xenia Forbes." Actually, these represented abbreviated, particularized descriptions of Imperial Easter Eggs designed by the firm of Faberge.

Wally needed these aids because, unlike Felix Ratliff, he was new to the market for Faberge objects. He had to do homework, rather than carry a picture and history of each item in his mind. Despite strong evidence that Felix Ratliff was older, richer, wiser, more charming, and more treacherous than himself, Wally proposed taking the other on. Not openly, of course. Perhaps Shakespeare's cynical observation that old age and treachery trump youth and talent every time was a bit of an exaggeration. Not *every* time, surely.

Wally had learned to recognize the hallmarks and initials associated with Faberge and his craftsmen, to discuss intelligently the range and quality of Faberge products, to judge the relative market values of various pieces, but these accomplishments would be counted small in the light of Mr. Ratliff's expertise, acquired over a period of more than fifty years.

On the other hand, there were several circumstances in Wally's favor. For one thing, he coveted these items more avidly than Ratliff, through whose hands so many precious objects had already passed. For another, the element of surprise lay with Wally. And finally, he had already contacted Rudi Anderson, not on Felix Ratliff's behalf, but his own.

None of these assets mitigated the danger of crossing Ratliff, of course. No one had ever called Ratliff a lovable person unless it was his mother, and of her opinion there was no public record. People had remarked approvingly on his glamor, his incredible luck, his intimacy with the "makers" of history, his ability to converse on almost any topic. But no one to date had publicly referred to him as generous or as devoted to anyone but himself.

In the past, rich Americans such as Ratliff, whose primary talent was making money, had seldom succeeded in capturing the hearts of their countrymen. However, today such individuals had far greater acceptance and were looked upon as icons, as figures to admire and emulate. Traditional virtues had declined in popularity while the general appetite for possessions and fabricated excitement had increased. Thus by the 1980's Felix Ratliff—although little more than a Marxist feasting on capitalists—enjoyed a certain vogue among journalists and other publicists that translated into occasional inclusion in "most admired man" polls.

Of course, Wally realized Ratliff was not beloved in the sense that Charles Lindberg or, on a different level, the Tsar were beloved. There was no awe, no mystic quality attached to him. Rather, the public was attracted to the fantasy of duplicating his wealth, of moving in his glamorous circles, of owning his seemingly innumerable "things." The public cared nothing for the real Felix Ratliff.

And Ratliff returned the public's indifference to his true self, returned their contempt. Wally knew this to be true because he once heard the man proclaim as much, after reading an editorial in a London news weekly questioning his business ethics. He dismissed the writer as "another cow among the lowly herd." All his life Ratliff had stayed a step ahead of almost everyone else—a circumstance that taught him no humility, gave him no hesitation. Wielding the power of the "almighty dollar" with great effect, he seemed oblivious to the likelihood that such power might constitute his epitaph. He saw himself rather as an initiate into the future. Exotic and contradictory as it seemed, Felix Ratliff, the lionized American capitalist, was convinced in his heart of Communism's ultimate victory. Thus his intimate association with the Soviet government and its espionage apparatus.

The role of profiteering prophet gave Ratliff the best of two worlds: the life style of the old and the good will of the new. Each advantage could be carried over from one world to the other.

Communist conviction—and Capitalist money—made Felix buoyant, among the most entertaining of men under the right conditions. Traveling with him, especially in Europe, had proven a truly memorable event for Wally. The man knew so many places, so much history, had so few restrictions on where he could go or not go. He could discourse as fluently on Greek vineyards as on pre-Druidic megaliths or Restoration drama. Almost anywhere on the continent or in the British Isles he could perform magic.

Wally always looked forward to meeting the fascinating people Ratliff included in his travels. This season's companions—the Kentucky Van Cleefs and their neighbor Georgia Beech—had broadened Wally's horizons in many ways. Mindful of their special interests, Ratliff had included stables, races, hunts, horse sales, and equestrian sculpture on the itinerary, with ready commentary for all. However, for reasons best known to himself—perhaps his considerable age—he had not actually joined a hunt.

Their joint travels were scheduled to end the Saturday on which the *Queen Anne* docked in Oslo, but upon learning that Felix intended to linger in the Norwegian capital, his companions decided to extend their vacation, too. If this election displeased Ratliff, he did not show it. He merely informed them he had business in Oslo and would necessarily absent himself from most of their activities. Only Wally knew that his business involved Faberge Eggs.

The Van Cleefs and Georgia perfectly understood. They would be on their own, as on the "free" day in Copenhagen or the day they hunted boar in Croatia. Amicably they fended for themselves and purchased various maps and guidebooks, to be added to their considerable other luggage, which included such extras as gun cases and boot boxes.

Wally was settled in the hotel when the other four arrived in Oslo late Saturday afternoon and were met by a limousine—a luxury regularly afforded by Ratliff. He made no secret of the fact that he was already acquainted with the chauffeur, as had happened several times during the trip. On the way in from Fornebu, Ratliff advised the others of likely restaurants for dining in Oslo that evening, since he himself had a business engagement.

Presumably tired from their travels, the Kentuckians and Georgia chose to eat in the hotel. This freed Wally and Felix to meet in a nearby restaurant for a light dinner. Later Wally joined Georgia and the Van Cleefs in venturing outside for an evening walk, an activity their guidebooks had pronounced safe in Oslo at any hour. After saying goodnight to them, Wally ventured down to the hotel bar and so by chance observed Felix conversing earnestly with three men at a corner table. He was perturbed that Ratliff seemed to be conducting business without him. After all, the success of his plan depended on knowing his employer's every move.

CHAPTER 9

▼

The following morning Georgia Beech found herself alone at breakfast, a situation she often experienced at home because of her husband's illness, which required early morning treatments. She had grown to appreciate the "lone time," as she called it, for it allowed her an uninterrupted hour to reflect on earlier events and to plan for later ones. She was particularly enjoying this particular Sunday morning alone, free from the hectic world that had swallowed her up in what was beginning to seem like an endless journey across Eastern Europe and Scandinavia.

She had no sooner completed this thought than Wally Macleod entered the dining room, looked around, spotted her, and came over to speak. She would have preferred being alone some while longer, but, gracious in that old-fashioned Southern way, she invited Wally to dine with her. They conversed amiably, without much real interest in each other's concerns, until he brought the conversation around to "Hamlet's castle."

"Speaking of Helsingør, Jon Olsen's in Oslo. Did you know that?"

"Olsen? Oh, the tall man we met touring the castle."

"Precisely."

"Did you get in trouble including me on that tour? I don't imagine the cruise people appreciated it."

"Oh, hell, they never knew. Walk up to one of their buses and they assume you're from the ship."

"I thought Mr. Olsen was on the cruise."

"Well, he's off now."

"Like you?" she asked, her luminous eyes gleaming.

"Like me." He added after a pause, "I'd like you to find out what he's up to."

"Me?" She laughed, possibly to disguise annoyance.

"It wouldn't hurt to look him up." When she did not respond, he continued, "I want to keep tabs on him. He's indirectly involved in a matter of concern to Felix. I know Mr. Ratliff would consider it a favor if he were a bit distracted, and…well, you're just the body to occupy his time."

"I am?"

"Come on, Georgia! If not for Felix, do it for me."

"But which is it, Wally, spying or keeping him busy?"

"Keeping him out of trouble."

Perhaps he had selected the right words, for she answered, "Well, I'll think about it." She then turned the conversation to other topics.

About an hour later, after consulting the Van Cleefs on the matter, Georgia decided perhaps she did owe Felix a favor, after all the kindnesses he had shown on the trip. She made a telephone call to Jon Olsen's hotel room. After several rings, a woman's voice answered. Georgia held the handset at a distance and looked at it questioningly before bringing it closer and saying, "I thought I was calling Jon Olsen."

"He's out," replied the voice.

"When do you expect him in?"

"I don't know."

"You're not the maid, are you?"

"I don't think that's any of your business!" the voice announced.

Again Georgia held the telephone away from her, to gain perspective, as it were, before answering. "Honey, I don't care if you're Joan of

Arc. I just want to leave a message. Tell him Georgia Beech called. Just a second, I'll give you my number."

"Georgia Peach?"

"Beech. 'B' as in 'Brazos.'"

"What's a Brazos?"

Georgia wondered if the woman was a smart aleck or merely deranged. "It's a metal cleaner," she added dryly.

"Oh!"

She hurriedly gave her hotel number, and added, "You got that?"

"Confirmed. Have you known Mr. Olsen long?"

"I don't think that's any of *your* business!" Georgia took some pleasure repeating the earlier declaration, but her jibe went unheeded.

"I met him yesterday," the voice continued.

"That's an event he's certain to remember!" She regretted the catty response the moment she uttered it, but the woman was completely unfazed.

"What do you want with Jon?"

Georgia decided the conversation was a lost cause. "Honey, I'd love to keep chatting, but the tub's running over. Adios," she said, and hung up.

She sat very still for a moment, feeling disoriented, almost dizzy at having reached a woman at Jon's hotel room fairly early in the morning. She recalled the trip to Helsingør with him and decided she wasn't so much offended as surprised. She had attributed certain characteristics to the man, characteristics not really compatible with having a woman the first night he hit town!

There came a tap on the connecting door, and her friend Deborah Van Cleef peeked in. "What'd he say?" she asked, when she spotted Georgia by the phone.

"Looks like there'll be just the three of us tonight."

"He's busy?" inquired Deborah, coming in.

"Chances are. A woman answered the phone."

Deborah's eyebrows shot up. "Hey! He's a fast worker, huh? Well, men're all the same, poor toads." She went up to the mirror on the bathroom door and began patting her hair in place. "I declare, I thought I combed this concoction."

Georgia eased herself from the bed and walked to the window overlooking the park. Pushing aside the glass curtain, she gazed at the verdant scene below while thinking of another time, of an overcast day at Kronborg castle.

After a moment Deborah announced, "Well, you know better than any what they're after. Men, I mean."

"They're after many things," Georgia said absently.

"Bother! They're after sex, Georgia Beech. Even the bright ones have one-track minds."

Still looking out the window, she answered, "Not necessarily. I've always believed that when men can manage to get away from us, they're generally delighted. They're sometimes on 'tracks' that don't include us." Now she turned to Deborah. "I don't believe most women realize that."

"I know you're talkin' silly, under the circumstances. Since we've lost your escort to naked lust."

Georgia laughed, and then, remembering suddenly, she said, "She called me 'Peach.'"

"Please, what are we talkin' about?"

"The woman on Jon's phone. She repeated my name as 'Peach.' 'Georgia Peach.' If only you knew the times someone's made a joke of that! Except she wasn't joking."

"She wasn't?"

"She was funny, but I don't think she's got a sense of humor."

"Just why are we psychoanalyzing her?" Deborah inquired.

Georgia thought a moment before acknowledging, "She kind of irked me, I guess."

"I don't see why a strange woman in a strange man's room should irk anybody!"

"Oh, no? How would *you* respond to 'What do you want with Jon?'"

"She said that? Shameless hussy! Well, I think I'd answer something like, 'Darlin', what does anybody want with such a lovely hunk of man!'" As Deborah spoke these last words, she put her hands on her hips and gave Georgia a significant stare.

Laughing, Georgia replied, "Damn good question! Let's go buy a fur hat!"

CHAPTER 10

▼

Before flying to Oslo, Violet had made contact with her old friend, the Countess of Dahlmark. The Countess, permanently imbedded in her villa outside Stockholm, could nonetheless supply the very latest in rumor, gossip, and innuendo from every corner of the globe. According to the Countess' sources, various officials were displaying considerable though discreet interest in the disposition of Yelena Anderson's estate. Perhaps most interested were the Russians!

The Countess reported furthermore that Felix Ratliff had made inquiries of the Norwegian authorities concerning the will. And my! how interesting that was! If the Countess recalled correctly, and she invariably did, Felix Ratliff had made a fortune selling Russian art works. In fact, he had proven so very successful in this regard that one must credit him with either incredibly good luck or, more likely, employment as an agent of the Soviet government.

"Felix Ratliff is not like your dear father," the Countess wrote, "who lost his chemise on Faberge and ikons." One could always tell when the Countess had been consulting her engagingly eccentric Swedish-English slang dictionary. "Although I enjoy the man personally, Felix has the morals of a snake," she finished.

Of Felix Ratliff's morals—or, rather, the lack thereof—Violet had no doubt. In the late '20's and early '30's, while Henrik Strasser was selling Russian masterpieces from his private collection to shore up his business, Ratliff's transactions featured one after another painting or *object d'art* miraculously freed from Soviet captivity and sold in America. There were Yusupov oils and Kelch jewels and Faberge Easter Eggs, all underpriced compared with afterwards, but netting Ratliff a substantial profit.

Ratliff managed to delicately circumvent questions as to whom the objects offered for sale truly belonged. After all, they had been confiscated in a revolution, had presumably passed from proletarian hand to proletarian hand, ultimately to reach Felix Ratliff's galleries. Might not these works still belong to the surviving Yusupovs, Kelches, and Romanovs? Short of that, were they not the revolutionary government's? Did Ratliff have them on consignment? His successes fed the art-world rumors that Lenin and Stalin had facilitated his transactions with the Soviet bureaucracy.

Such questions, of course, did not interfere with the operations of Felix Ratliff, who grew rich while working for Soviet-American "cultural exchange" and "better understanding." His capitalist empire expanded to the point that by the 1980's he sat on numerous corporate boards and received considerable media attention, especially in connection with promotional efforts for international peace and friendship. Several United States Presidents had given him audience, and more than one Soviet Party Chairmen had feted him.

The news of Ratliff's interest in Yelena's estate piqued Violet's curiosity, healthy by any standards. Surely he would not bother himself with a few picture frames and carved animals! He must therefore be after the "lost" Imperial Easter Eggs, of which there were eight by some counts, ten by others.

At some time or other, Violet's father told her the provenance of the Eggs in Yelena's possession. All Imperial Eggs were ordered from the firm of Faberge by Tsar Alexander III or Tsar Nicholas II for either wife or mother. Of all the Eggs, only one left Russia with its owner, the dowager empress. The Soviet government eventually retained ten, whereas most of the rest found their way to the West sooner or later.

Violet had herself seen three Faberge Eggs on that day long ago when her family called on Yelena in Christiania. She did not so much remember how they looked, as hearing about them from her parents afterwards. Yet she perfectly recalled the tiny music box inside one of the Eggs. Enameled, bejeweled, exquisite, it played a gay Chopin mazurka.

Yelena's Eggs had two separate origins: her association with Faberge and her legendary beauty. The Tsar never saw the Egg made from Karelian birch and dated 1917. By then, he had abdicated and existed as a virtual prisoner. The birch Egg remained unclaimed in Yelena's father's workshop. She simply—or, more probably, not so simply—took it with her upon fleeing Russia.

At least two other Eggs were placed in her hands by a Grand Duke whose son had become her lover. The Tsarina herself, from her captivity at Tsarskoe Selo, had slipped the Eggs to the Grand Duke, and he, prior to his arrest and execution, passed the treasures to Yelena. The Prince was to have joined her in the West later, but the revolution devoured him.

At the time of the Strassers' call on Yelena Anderson, she maintained she had no right to sell the Imperial Eggs. Official Soviet reports of the Prince and Grand Duke's executions might not be true. The death of the Tsar himself might be a fabrication. But even had these noblemen died as related—and the Prince, most brutally—the Imperial Eggs belonged to the Tsar's nearest heirs, to surviving Romanovs.

That was the position Yelena took in 1925, and possibly long afterwards. The Countess of Dahlmark remembered seeing the "jade" Egg at Yelena's almost 20 years later. And not long before the Nazi occupation, Yelena debated taking herself and her collection to neutral Sweden, once the Germans attacked Norway.

All these bits and pieces from Yelena's life had come to Violet's knowledge through her family and friends, or from Yelena herself after the occupation. Yet while the related events seemed correct, Violet wondered about that day in Christiania so many years ago. She had distinctly received the impression then that sale of the Eggs somehow depended upon the missing Mr. Anderson. Yet how so, if the Grand Duke entrusted them to Yelena?

And how was it Violet saw no sign of the Eggs on her subsequent visit? Even her romantic obsession with Tryggvi could not blind her to anything so distinctive as an Imperial Russian Egg! In fact, she had examined the windowed cabinets and mirrored étagères in Yelena's rooms for the express purpose of again viewing the Eggs and imperial portraits. She had seen only the latter.

Had the Nazis confiscated the Eggs? Had Yelena stored them in a bank vault? Or had she perhaps hidden them from friend and enemy alike?

On their last occasion together, Violet had taken tea with Yelena at the end of a lovely summer's day. Of the dozens of questions she wanted to ask Yelena, she had finally asked only one: "What became of the 'missing' Faberge Eggs?"

All Yelena had said was, "They can be found."

Such a peculiar way to respond, Violet reflected now. Yes, peculiar indeed.

CHAPTER 11

▼

Violet was the first to enter Yelena's house on Oscars Gate Sunday morning. As on previous visits, the air seemed close, so she opened windows and shutters freely. It promised to be a glorious day—bright, clear, and warm. Across the way, purple petunias nodded sedately in the breeze, and curled cats stirred languidly in the sun.

Regretting the need to work inside, Violet forced herself to face the interior of Yelena's house, not the same interior she remembered from childhood, nor even from her second visit. Whitewash replaced wallpaper in the larger downstairs rooms, and much of the furniture had changed. Most disappointing of all, there were no Imperial Easter Eggs.

"They can be found," Yelena had said. Yet thus far, neither Violet nor Rudi nor Xenia had come upon a single one. It had occurred to Violet that her cousins might have found and "lost" the Eggs prior to her own appearance on the scene, and that others—Norwegian officials or possibly American Embassy personnel—may have had similar opportunities for theft. But as she equally disliked the ideas of cheating relatives and thieving strangers, she pretended not to have thought of them. Besides, almost all the Eggs had survived the destructive chaos of the Russian Revolution, and surely their greater fame and higher value today protected them even more from lesser threats.

Their enhanced worth was real. To beauty and fancy and fashion had been added the mystery of vanished times, of fallen aristocracy, of a cellar massacre. Alas, there was ample proof that tragic and macabre associations stimulate human interest in just about anything. And the Romanov slaughter at Ekaterinburg followed a singularly grisly course, with guns and bayonets and blood and amputations and acid and fire and mine shafts. She really hated to think about it!

Imagining Faberge's delivery of the Eggs at Easter was far more pleasant. She liked to think of the Tsarina, in corseted splendor, wearing a diamond tiara and taking tea in a Crimean palace garden. Suddenly a servant tremulously announces, "Monsieur Carl Faberge." He shows no dust from the long trip, because he has changed his clothes. He bears a Faberge case, oyster white and elliptical in shape. He places it in the Tsarina's expectant hands.

She opens it, and there, inside, is her world: shimmering, commanding, delicately balanced, fully detailed. She takes the Egg from its case, places it on the tea table and opens it by pressing a diamond button that Faberge points out to her. At the lovely surprise within, she clasps her hands like a child.

Violet herself smiled, as she fancied the Tsarina's delight, for delight it must have been on some twenty Easters. And for the Tsar's mother, the Dowager Empress Marie Feodorovna, such delight recurred for thirty-two years—to end like all things, except that all things do not end so bloodily.

With a sigh, Violet glanced at Yelena's desk, at the photograph of her prince in his Faberge picture frame. He, too, came to a gruesome end of bayonets and mine shafts; whereas in this photograph he gazed languidly, a subtle smile of contentment forever on his lips, an everlasting air of command in the confident tilt of his head.

And Yelena? What tortures had she suffered? Neither Violet nor Rudi knew. They had talked about her escape without knowing its details. Nor had they learned anything significant about it from the correspondence and other records in Yelena's house. Actually, only

Rudi and Xenia were going through those documents, since Violet read only two languages besides her own, whereas her cousins managed Russian, Swedish, Finnish, Norwegian, German, English and French—all the languages Yelena used.

This disparity between her few languages and their many caused Violet a mild unease. She certainly regretted her nephew Jon's typically American ignorance of all foreign tongues! What had Hia been thinking of, to marry into so insular a family as the Olsens of Minnesota! Furs and forests indeed! And all because of some happy-go-lucky 19th century trapper too tall for his own good! Jon would never have grown so outlandishly big, had he been pure Strasser rather than mixed Olsen. A shame, of course, that people couldn't be pure Strasser.

Well, there was nothing for it. Jon might have a splendid brain, but it dealt exclusively in English and from an unseemly six-and-a-half-foot frame. So she could either bring him up to date on her lack of discoveries and hope he might thereby receive a flash of inspiration, or she could ask him to catalogue items—a task she hated herself. Or he could…

"Do you always leave doors unlocked?"

Jumping at the sound of her nephew's voice so near, she answered tartly, "You shouldn't sneak up on people!"

"It's a good idea to latch doors, even in Norway."

She rather sniffed. "What happened to you last night?"

"Were we supposed to meet?" he countered, while shucking off his jacket. "I thought you were having dinner with Rudi and Xenia." He placed the coat on the back of a chair. "I really can't remember."

"Why can't you remember?"

"A little too much to drink."

"Good Heavens! You didn't abandon that pretty girl on some street!" Violet exclaimed. She held a highly skeptical view of anyone's behavior when drunk.

"Of course not. She's fast asleep."

"And how would you know that?"

"Well, I don't knew it for an absolute certainty, Aunt Violet."

"I see," she said, thinking she all too easily saw more than she cared to. She looked at him with mounting doubt as, towering before her, he rolled up his shirtsleeves. "Are you going to do some plumbing or something?"

"If you like."

"Well, let me tell you you'll do nothing of the sort!"

Perhaps he had been teasing, because he looked almost as if he smiled, while making no motion to move. "What's the plan, then?"

"That's the trouble. I can't think of one. We've been all through the house, and there's no sign of an Egg."

"When you say 'all through the house,' what do you mean?"

"Why, I mean drawers, cabinets, containers. Like burglars looking for loot."

"Under carpets?"

"Of course not!"

"Inside water closets?" he went on, uncowed.

"Heavens no!" And then, because she imagined he looked smug, she added, "Maybe you'd like to make your own search!"

"Hm. Well, the ceilings aren't very high."

"I'm sure all ceilings are low to you!" she retorted.

"Did Yelena have carpeting when you visited before?"

"Oak floors with rugs."

He moved to a corner of the room, knelt, and at once, expertly wielding a pocketknife, began tearing up the carpet.

"Good heavens! What are you doing?"

"Checking for false flooring," he answered and, having pulled back a section of carpet, he pried up several floorboards with surprising ease.

Half expecting him to pluck forth an Imperial Egg for her gratified view, she postponed indignation over the destruction. Prepared equally to rejoice or condemn, she edged toward him. "What have you found?" she asked.

"Under flooring," he replied laconically and slapped the floorboards back in place before she quite reached him.

"You've made a shambles!"

"Some tacks will put it right. I'll get some tomorrow." He was smoothing the carpet down. "Meanwhile, I can move a cabinet over it, if you like."

"Don't touch the cabinets!"

He eyed her intently, then rose to his feet with a push of his hands against the floor. "All right."

"Jon, such extremes aren't necessary! And anyway, I want to say something before Rudi comes."

"What's that?"

She drew him after her to a window from which they could see the front porch. When she spoke, she fairly whispered, "Do you think we can trust Rudi? Suppose he found the Eggs before I got here!"

"If he did, you certainly can't trust him," he judged.

"But do you think it's likely?"

"Well, it's certainly possible."

"But likely? What do you think, Jon?"

"I think maybe Yelena didn't hide the Eggs here at all."

"Why do you say that?"

"Because you haven't found them. Because, from what you and the cousins said yesterday, no one's seen them for years. Not in this house, at any rate."

"That's not enough to go on," she objected.

"Of course, I can take the place apart—not everything, you understand, but anything not structural. Except that using our wits ought to prove more productive. She most likely left a clue somewhere."

"I've thought of that. And also, that finding a clue's easier for Rudi and Xenia, with all their languages."

There came a silence. Violet now sat behind the desk while Jon sat on the edge facing her, his long legs stretched well beyond the back of her chair. "Don't you find it odd that Yelena had two desks?" she asked, more to break the silence than to solicit information. "There's another in her dressing room."

"Not really. I have two desks in my upstairs room at home. One is for business—engineering drawings, blueprints, and so forth. The other has my computer and personal correspondence. I don't think it's very unusual these days."

She was tempted to point out that Yelena hadn't lived in "these days," but thought better of it. She watched him surveying the room in a leisurely manner, apparently deep in thought, and she made an impatient gesture. "So! Where—how—do we look for a clue?"

"As I understand, she didn't die here, in this house."

"No. She was walking."

"In the street out front?"

"No. On Bygdøy."

"What's Bygdøy?" he asked.

"It's where they have the Viking ships. Sort of an island."

"Close by?"

"Oh, a distance, as I remember. But Yelena always had stamina. Imagine leaving Russia on foot!"

Jon leaned over and pulled a map from the pocket of his jacket, hanging on Violet's chair. He placed the map in front of her and said, "Show me."

"I can't see without my glasses." Once this obstacle had been overcome, she pointed out Oscars Gate and then Bygdøy. The distance between looked to be about two miles.

"Have you seen where she died, the exact spot?" he inquired.

"No. I haven't been out there."

"Was she going to visit somebody, do you know?"

"I haven't asked."

Again there came a silence. He ended it by taking a new tack. "What about correspondence, records?"

"Rudi's discovered nothing—that is, nothing important about Eggs."

"Mm. It wouldn't necessarily be straight out. Has he listed what he's found?"

"I'm not sure. You'll have to ask him. Or Xenia. Right now she's doing most of it."

"Okay."

Violet felt like a child put down by its elders. Here she had done none of the things her nephew seemed to consider important. The fact this was an Easter Egg hunt simply heightened her sense of juvenility, as did, of course, the fact that Jon was Hia's son. As long as she lived, Hia had borne a bland, parental superiority towards Little Sister Violet—Violet the spinster.

She reminded herself that Hia never possessed much of the logic she had bequeathed to her son. Rather, she persuaded and dominated through incredible, self-assured narrow-mindedness. Violet could still see the convinced set of Hia's lips, could still hear the Jovian placidity of Hia's tone. With such a bullheaded example of womankind before him, no wonder Jon never married!

She became conscious of her nephew's having spoken. "What did you say?"

"Do you want me to search? I'll be careful."

"Well…" She looked at the corner where he had pulled up the carpet. It didn't seem so bad in comparison with the memory of Hia. "I suppose you might take a look around. Just don't touch any of the valuables!"

He said, "You'll have to tell me what's different from before. We'll just walk about, and you'll point out the changes." He picked up a note pad from the desk.

They went from room to room—she, straining her memory to recall how things had looked to her as a child and then, later on, as Tryggvi's would-be beloved. The procedure upset her equilibrium, what with the intervening years, regrets about Tryggvi, and no prior familiarity whatsoever with several of the rooms. "I can't possibly help you here!" she exclaimed testily of Yelena's room. "I never saw it!"

Unperturbed, Jon asked, "When you searched in here, where did you look?"

"The closets, of course—rather thoroughly. But certainly not her box springs!"

It was during the casing of Yelena's room that Rudi and Xenia let themselves into the house and called up to Violet. Seeing Jon, too, at the top of the stairs, the couple came up. Xenia was not impeded a whit by the very high heels she wore, while Rudi moved more slowly in loafers. An awkward silence succeeded the general greetings. Next followed an exchange about Jon's absence from the previous night's dinner. Neither Xenia nor Rudi inquired about Anna.

In due course it was decided that Jon should consult both his cousins in the matter of Yelena's correspondence and records. Thus while Violet and Xenia busied themselves with a review of Yelena's various articles of clothing, Rudi described the sundry financial and property records. Later, Xenia became Jon's instructor, while Rudi and Violet resumed cataloguing Yelena's collection. Throughout these endeavors, Violet kept a watchful eye on the three of them. It occurred to her that the remnants of her family, once spread broadly through the world, was now gathered in Yelena Anderson's bedroom.

Jon listened attentively as Xenia described Yelena's correspondence as substantial in the 1920's and most of the '30's, but dwindling thereafter. Upon his questioning, she enumerated several recurrent themes in the correspondence: the Russian Revolution, émigrés' affairs, Ingmar Anderson, developments in art and literature. Jon wrote them down.

"And to whom did she write?"

Xenia named émigrés, Andersons, art dealers, and assorted other merchants. She mentioned the Countess of Dahlmark, Marshal Mannerheim, two bankers, and a British earl. She told of a copy of a letter to Felix Ratliff in which Yelena declined to sell an Egg to him.

"What was the date of that?" Violet asked from across the room.

They looked over at her, apparently surprised she was paying attention to their conversation.

"Shortly after ze war," Xenia replied.

"World War Two?" asked Jon.

"Zat war."

"And have you separated the letters by correspondent?"

"Not exactly, my darlink. Was I supposed to?" Xenia batted her mascara'd lashes at Jon and smoothed the close-fitting waist of her fashionable dress. Violet frowned but pretended not to notice.

"How did you separate them?"

"Yelena already has everyzink in such order."

"What order?"

"By year, by topic," she said. "All ze banking togezzer in one pot, ze personal correspondence by person in another." She studied him a moment. "But do you know, Jon, you should sometimes smile? Such a handsome man—but never ze smile."

Possibly he did smile, although the change in his expression was too slight for Xenia—or Violet—to notice. "Show me the correspondence," he directed, and they moved into Elena's dressing room, which contained her writing desk. Violet continued to catalog with Rudi at the opposite corner of the bedroom, annoyed that Jon and Xenia were no longer in her line of sight or within hearing.

Almost an hour passed, and Violet's curiosity grew unbearable. Jumping up, she walked to the end of the bedroom, thence into Yelena's dressing room. She was extremely annoyed to find her nephew and Xenia seated chummily on the floor of the sunny room, the boxes of letters unattended in front of them as Xenia read Jon's palm!

Looking up as Violet bit her lip at this frivolous activity, Jon quickly said to his companion, "Just a minute. Here's Aunt Violet."

Xenia, without letting go his hand, twisted to see Violet. "We've been workink so hard! Just see what we've accomplished: our little elastics!" and with her free hand she snapped one of the rubber bands holding and segregating Yelena's letters in unequal bunches.

"Quite marvelous," said Violet dryly.

"Next we weigh zem."

"Oh, splendid!" Violet replied with undiminished dryness.

"It will tell us—what will it tell us?" Xenia said, turning to Jon again.

Violet lost her temper. "It'll tell us how much time's been wasted!" she declared in rather ringing tones.

While Xenia looked at her with surprise, Jon extricated his hand and stood up quickly. "Please calm down. Would you like a glass of water?"

She glowered at him. "I need assistance, not parlor games!" she asserted.

"My efforts haven't been spectacular, I know." He spoke calmly, entirely without defensiveness, which annoyed Violet even more.

She glanced down at Xenia, still interested in the conversation, still cross-legged on the floor. "I don't see a connection between help and palm reading," Violet fumed.

"Please. Come with me," Jon said, and guided her from the room. A little beyond Xenia's hearing he continued quietly, "Don't upset yourself, Aunt Violet. We'll talk later."

"About rubber bands!"

"In a way. But later," he repeated, with a last, knowing look at her before he returned to Xenia, to whom Violet heard him say, "Tell me about my heart line."

Violet stamped her foot in frustration. They would never find the Imperial Easter Eggs through palmistry and rubber bands! Oh, why didn't he *do* something! And Xenia, the flirt! Had she nothing better to do than make goo-goo eyes at a confirmed bachelor half her age? It was absurd!

As she returned to Elena's bedroom, Rudi said, "Did you notice? The carpet's pulled up in the next room! What does it mean?"

"It means my nephew's a vandal!" she snapped.

CHAPTER 12

▼

Anna Nygaard put in an appearance at Yelena's house on Oscars Gate shortly before noon. Her clothes—the same as yesterday's—looked slightly mussed, but every shampooed hair was in place. She wore dark glasses, which she did not remove upon entering the house. She immediately asked for Jon, and Violet directed her to the dressing room where he and Xenia toiled. Anna sensed Violet appraising yesterday's clothing with an unapproving eye.

Before long, Anna, Xenia, and Jon took their leave, having informed the others of their plan to walk to Bygdøy to see how long it might have taken Yelena to reach the spot where she died, which Anna could identify. Rudi and Violet had declined to participate in the experiment, but Xenia, having declared she had climbed the Pyrenees in heels higher than the ones she now wore, had accepted Anna's invitation with alacrity. Thus, the three set out from Oscars Gate as a unit.

In Oslo, as in Leningrad, the weather was uncommonly warm. As a result, Jon, his shirtsleeves rolled up, carried his jacket slung over one shoulder. The ladies, more lightly dressed, had no such burden, but only their handbags to manage.

A mild breeze intermittently caught at Xenia's full skirt and Anna's ad-perfect hair, as the three proceeded south in a generally downhill mode. Anna noted approvingly Jon's efforts to put himself always closest to the curb in the manner many Americans had been taught as children. The practice, she knew, stemmed from medieval times and the linkage between street gutters and slopjars. In spite of his efforts, however, Xenia continually migrated to the outside—apparently to be next to him—so Anna suggested that he walk between them. Thus he gave up his attempt to observe social custom in deference to his companions' preference.

They went on with Jon in the middle, sometimes with a lady clinging to each arm, as when they paused to admire or otherwise note some part of their surroundings, or when they encountered uneven flagstones. Anna found it remarkable how Xenia navigated across everything: cobbles, ditches, soft ground, whatever. She showed every indication not only of having been able to climb the Pyrenees in three-inch heels, but Mount Everest as well.

The breeze blew lightly, the sun shone brightly, as they continued their gradual descent toward the fjord along neat, narrow streets and modern, wider ones. They saw homes and embassies, shops and hotels on their passage to the Drammensveien, which ran parallel to the unseen shore. As the distance mounted, they adopted a faster pace in acknowledgment of the lesser, steadier gradient and in expectation of Bygdøy somewhere ahead.

Meanwhile, conversation had been almost continuous and quite lively. Xenia told them about fleeing across Eastern Europe and of her conversion from the Orthodox Church to astrology—the latter eliciting playfully derisive comments from the others. Jon described the geology of fjords and the orientation of harbor cities—which caused the ladies to peer around him and exchange questioning looks. Anna described certain Norwegian folk customs and a telephone communication from a person calling herself Georgia Peach—which resulted in an audible intake of breath by her companions, followed by general silence.

At the particular moment Anna mentioned Georgia, they were arm-in-arm like the three musketeers. When he looked into her upturned eyes, she wondered what he read there.

"'Beech,'" was all he said, but she noticed he walked slightly more slowly, so obliging them to do the same.

"Are you in love with her?" Anna asked in her direct, disorienting way.

He mumbled something about being too old for that sort of thing and charged the subject. Anna decided not to pursue the issue further—not with Xenia hanging onto every word.

They broke into the open at last, where an arm of the sea reached its end and a major highway twisted along the edge. Anna pointed out the way to Bygdøy, and, dodging traffic, they reached the indicated side of both road and fjord. Once across, they lost the highway and traffic in a matter of seconds by following a side road. Almost immediately they found themselves in a pastoral setting.

Evidently Xenia had never taken this route in previous visits to Oslo, for she exclaimed, "But what is zis? We're in ze country?"

"This is where Yelena died," returned Anna. "I'll show you." She led them down a path, lined with undulating willows, and through a gate into a meadow. They tramped through grass, along the fence, and came to a bench, shaded by one of the nearby trees.

"Here," she said, touching the bench. "Of course, her body fell to the ground." She indicated the general area with her foot. "A friend found her an hour or so later. Apparently she was walking to his house for a visit and never showed up."

"Who was this friend?"

"Someone she knew before the Revolution, I imagine." Anna looked at him brightly.

"Where was she buried?" Jon asked.

"That's one of the oddities of this case," Anna replied. "Nobody seems to know—unless the friend does." She then looked pointedly at Xenia. "Do you know?"

"I know nozzing," she replied quickly.

Jon laid his coat on the bench and scanned the meadow, the whole 180-degree arc. "Did she come here often? Does anyone know?"

"Just sometimes. For a walk—or to visit her friend," Anna answered,

"A hefty walk for a woman of eighty."

"A woman who spent months walking out of Russia? I think not."

Staring at Anna, he gave a suppressed sound between a sigh and a cough before inquiring, "Was this her usual destination, do you know?"

Xenia interjected, "What if she buried ze Eggs here!"

"Then we'll need luck and a bulldozer," Jon commented dryly. "What about it, Anna? Did Yelena ever go farther?"

"Her friend lived on Huk terrasse. Sometimes they had tea together, then Yelena would take the ferry home."

"The ferry doesn't go to Oscars Gate?" Jon inquired."

"It docks near the Radhuset. I'll show you on the way back."

"Did you talk to zis friend of Yelena's?"

Anna turned to face Xenia. "No, but the Norwegian police did. I saw the report." She then turned to Jon. "The friend claimed to know nothing about the Eggs. He's in Switzerland now," she added, as if one fact explained the other.

"So! Ze Eggs could be anywhere on zis island?"

"Peninsula," corrected Anna.

Meanwhile, Jon had picked up his jacket. "Let's continue to this friend's house and then find something to eat," he suggested.

But on the way, they took a wrong turn and found themselves at the Viking ships museum. Because Jon regarded this accident as serendipity at its finest, they toured the museum, whose sheer white walls dramatically offset the dark woods of the menacingly graceful Viking ships.

As happens in museums, each wandered off in different directions, sometimes catching up to or passing one another as they studied the exhibits. Anna, who had seen the ships a number of times, finished earlier than the others. She was about to exit onto the grounds, when Jon took her by the arm. "Just a minute," he said.

A clinical look came at once to her eyes, and she answered, in an accusing sort of way, "I know what you want!"

He let go of her arm. "Do you?"

"You want that woman's number!"

He said nothing

"Well, I didn't memorize it. I wrote it down."

"Thank you."

"But I'm much better for you! You'll see! We're destined for one another!"

"I'm old enough to be…"

"Don't give me that crap!" Anna commanded.

"Anna, it's…"

"It's a new age, that's what!"

"It's a silly obsession!" he managed to squeeze in.

"You'll see!" she threatened, almost as effectively as the looming prow of the nearest Viking ship.

"There have to be dozens of young men who…"

"Oh, shove it up your young men!" she declared in tones sufficiently loud that bystanders looked in their direction.

Anna stared them down, and without another word sailed away in stately fashion, her model's hair billowing lazily in her wake.

*   *   *   *

Jon watched Anna stride away, her dress swaying, her hair glinting as she passed under spotlights illuminating the Viking ships. Despite the scene she had just created, he could not help acknowledging that she certainly cut a fine figure. The bystanders must think him a fool to let her go.

Of course, he was furious with her for the thought implanted in the bystanders' minds, just as he was angry at her abandonment of all logic. There was no *reason* for her behavior; any more than there was a reason for her guessing correctly his interest in having Georgia's number. In short, she had stirred him up.

He wondered abstractly whether stirring him up might have been her objective. After all, although decidedly odd, she very evidently did not lack brains. She could be frighteningly perceptive as well as disconcertingly forward. She probably planned any conquest with the thoroughness of the German General Staff.

As to why she chose him, Jon couldn't fathom. Some illogical female fancy, perhaps. Or maybe it was one of those social trends, wherein unattached, fortyish American males were being pursued by much younger women across Europe. That was quite common in countries like Spain and Italy. Older, successful men—men who had sown their oats, hopefully—were considered the pick of the litter in such cultures. Or perhaps it was as simple as Freud maintained: for some young women, the father image did indeed prevail. But for all that, Jon didn't feel he'd really explained Anna's fancy.

Perhaps, as he'd originally accused, she had a "silly obsession," triggered by boredom or his unusual height or being drunk together or some similarly trivial consideration. Or perhaps, because he didn't look his age, she thought of him as younger than he was. Or perhaps she liked some quality special to him: his calmness, for instance, or his courtesy.

However that may be, Jon seethed as he went about the museum now. More significantly, he was not thinking of Georgia Beech. Whether looking at the elegant form of the grandly sinister ships or at the lesser artifacts in their glass cases, he kept hearing Anna's "Shove it!" driving everything else from his mind.

Not that he plotted revenge. Rather, there was a kind of shock in hearing such words from such lips, quite apart from the challenge in the words themselves, quite apart from their broadcast abroad. It was the unbecoming nature of her conduct that most stirred him up—its unseemliness, and his powerlessness before it.

After about ten minutes, Xenia intervened in his silent stewing by announcing her readiness to leave. They exchanged opinions such as "Majestic" and "In their way, terrifying" as they passed one of the ships on the way out, and Jon remarked that it was hard to believe the ships had actually been buried for centuries.

Xenia, who had been striding as nonchalantly as ever in her high heels—even after the miles and the standing around—suddenly stumbled. He reached out and steadied her, to encounter her eyes, looking fearfully at him. "Are you all right?" he asked, thinking she had hurt herself. She hastened to say it was nothing, nothing at all, and stepped out smartly to prove it.

Once outside, Anna acted as if nothing untoward had happened. She even bestowed on him one of her rare and tepid smiles. He forced himself to remain stoic, and off the three of them went in quest of Huk terrasse.

They found the street, a residential dead end with a storybook look to houses and gardens that evoked eternal summer, as if these dwellings existed for leisure. There were garden walls and flower boxes and half-timbering and casement windows. Xenia expressed her delight with a little squeak as they walked to the end of the terrasse.

"Which one belongs to Yelena's friend?" Jon asked, while reading the name on the closest door. "'Vaino.' Does that sound right?"

"I don't know," Anna replied.

He stopped walking and looked at her reproachfully. "You don't know?"

"No," she said, with a shrug and no explanation. She stood several feet away, as did Xenia.

He gazed off to his left, at the same time uttering a frustrated sigh. Apparently Anna had decided to be difficult.

"I have places to go and people to meet," Anna called cheerily over her shoulder as she began walking away.

He said "Damn!" under his breath and remained where he was.

Xenia, who had started to follow Anna, now paused and looked back. "Aren't you comink?"

"In a moment."

"We mustn't get lost!"

"I have the map."

"Ah!" She returned to him. "Ze map! Anna doesn't need one!" She laughed. "And we don't need her!"

"We'll catch up."

"Such a charmink street, n'es pas? Ze trees, ze flowers. It's like a fairy tale."

Together they admired the view, as Anna disappeared from sight. After studying the map for a moment, he offered Xenia his arm. "Let's go find her," he said, sounding confident of the outcome.

His confidence proved justified. As soon as they turned the corner, they saw her a block ahead. She had stopped at a kind of inn or restaurant. Looking back, seeing them, she waved and waited. As they came even with her, she announced, "We'll go in to lunch."

The restaurant featured smorgasbord and the weaker alcoholic beverages. Xenia and Jon made various selections, whereas Anna loaded her plate with rolls and sardines. Xenia chose wine, and the other two, beer.

After they were seated at a table, one lady on either side of Jon, Anna put forth the theory that, in the event Yelena had hidden the Eggs on Bygdøy, they were lost forever. "It's a very big place," she pointed out.

Xenia took exception in that, if the Swiss friend's house contained the Eggs, they were discoverable.

"He's not Swiss," contradicted Anna.

"Zat's what you said!"

"I said he's gone to Switzerland. He's got a Finnish name."

Jon contributed nothing to this debate, but listened and ate, until at one point Anna turned to him and advised, "I wouldn't bother with Bygdøy."

"Why not?"

"You have four days. Concentrate on what's possible."

Answering nothing, he looked at her with new respect and appeared to acknowledge her advancement from recalcitrant child to adulthood by pouring some beer from his bottle into her glass.

She seemed to take the action in a complementary way. In any case, she said, "Your acts of affection are so awesomely unshowy!"

When they had eaten, Anna led them to the shore, where a landing and small marina were located. Ferry times and prices were posted beside the window of a ticket booth. After buying their tickets, they had twenty minutes to wait and spent time drinking beer in the sun.

A launch arrived, and they boarded along with a few other passengers. They took the back bench with Jon once again in the middle. He folded his arms across his chest and stretched his legs into the center aisle.

Anna asked what they were going to do next, and he said he would be reporting back to his aunt.

"I'll go with you," she announced. "To help. I can't be with you tomorrow. I'll be working."

"Fine. Only I have to stop off at my hotel first, so you might like to go 'round with Xenia."

She favored him with one of her clinical looks. "I'll come with you," she said.

Once on the dock below the Radhuset, Xenia took off in the direction of the National Theatre, and the others toward Jon's hotel. Anna and he walked in silence, for the most part. Doubtless she was planning how to accompany him to his room, and he was at a loss as to how to prevent it. In that event, surrender might be his best tack.

"The number's on the table by the phone," she told him as he let her pass before him into the room. She went over to the table and picked up a piece of paper. "See." She waved it like bait.

Closing the door and taking a few paces into the room, he laid down his coat and folded his arms, to gaze at her steadily. "It's still your move," he said.

"There's no point if your heart's not in it, Jon."

"What do you mean?"

"I think you know."

He unfolded his arms. "Suppose you go powder your nose or something, while I make this call."

"Oh, you won't bother me at all!"

"I'd like to make the call by myself. Do you mind?"

"Certainly not! I won't listen. I'll hang my head out the window. She went to the window, opened it, and leaned far out.

She had won again. He made the best of it by crossing over to the table, picking up the paper and pocketing it. "Let's go," he said, tapping her shoulder.

She whirled around quickly, but he already was beyond her reach on his way to the door. "Wait!" He turned back.

"I'll go put on some lipstick," she said. "But first, kiss me."

"Anna!"

She reached out to him. "Please, kiss me."

Of course he did, and rather longer than he had intended. "What am I to do with you!" he murmured, smoothing her hair.

"Kiss me again!"

He did. This time she broke off the kiss herself and fled from him into the adjoining bath, meanwhile leaving him once again not thinking of Georgia Beech. He had to search his mind to recall why it was he had wanted Anna out of the room.

Feeling somewhat abashed upon remembering, he made the call, only to discover that Mrs. Beech did not answer. He left a message inviting her to dinner. Hanging up, he took time to get a leash on his emotions.

She opened the door to discover him seated on the edge of the bed. She sat down beside him and stroked his cheek along the scar. "When will you see her?" she asked mildly.

He patted her hand and very determinedly stood up. "Let's go," he said. "Aunt Violet's already on my back about getting something done."

"You must have a plan. What is it?"

"Come along and I'll tell you," he said, helping her up. He moved away too quickly for any successful temptation. "I assume the hangover's all gone?"

"Yes. Quite. The walk did me a world of good."

"Can you read German as well as Norwegian?"

"Oh, yes. Dutch and Swedish, too."

He looked at his watch. "Then let's get over to Yelena's."

∗   ∗   ∗   ∗

They found Violet in Yelena's study, alone and somewhat distant in manner. As Xenia had yet to turn up again, and Rudi had left three hours before on some excuse, Violet may have nursed resentment at solo martyrdom in the cause of closing Yelena's estate. However, she uttered no word of reproach.

Jon set Anna to work on the correspondence in the back room and then came up front again to speak to his aunt. He began explaining his plan for finding the Eggs. It rested on the principle implicit in Anna's recommendation, namely, the principle for winning games involving chance: play the way the cards must lie to win the game.

His plan assumed that Yelena left a clue, even an explicit message. They must look for it. Anna would read through as much of the correspondence as she could, starting with the largest packets, from the date in 1939 when the Countess of Dahlmark last saw any of Yelena's Eggs.

Tomorrow, with Anna back at work, Violet and the cousins would pursue the rest of the post-1939 correspondence. Meanwhile he and Violet would look about the house for clues.

At this point, he eyed Violet intently, for she seemed singularly without interest in what he had been saying. "Is something wrong?" he asked. "Don't you like the plan?"

"Yes, yes." She said it abstractedly, as it were, not seeming to care what question he asked. And then she murmured, "What do we really know of Yelena!"

She was sitting at the large desk she had occupied that morning. "Something is wrong," Jon said. What is it?" He began moving around the desk, to stop beside her.

"How can I tell you of the past, of its duality: how it lives on, but never again?" Her big, black eyes stared up at him, and she spoke in almost a whisper. "You can't possibly understand how it was in Oslo, when Oslo was Christiania. I can no longer understand myself. But I saw an apparition here. Here, in this very house."

"I know. You've told me about it."

"It was right over there!" she said, extending her arm and pointing toward the hall. The sudden energy in her voice made him look where she pointed. He may have expected to see the apparition, but what he saw was a doorway without a door. From somewhere in the rear of the house, light penetrated to this opening and played with the shadows there. "Yelena understood that I saw the apparition that day. I'm sure of it! Why else would I have been named an heir? Souls of the deceased are visible to only a few."

He took his time bringing his eyes back to bear on her. When he did so, he asked, "Have you seen it again?"

She continued as if he had not spoken. "I've always wanted to know who the apparition was. Because I don't believe in ghosts, not even in hallucinations."

"You probably saw someone all right. But after so long, we're not likely to know who."

She whispered again, motioning him to lean closer. "While you were at Bygdøy, I found my apparition!"

"What do you mean!"

"Shh! Tell no one!" She carefully eased open the desk drawer and brought out a photograph, which she handed to Jon with the words, "This is my apparition!"

He looked at the unframed portrait of a young man, bearded and grave, in some kind of uniform. Jon flipped it over and read the legend on the back: Jager Vaino 1920.

He suddenly recalled the nameplate he'd seen earlier in the day. "Vaino! Aunt Violet, that's the name of Yelena's friend on Bygdøy!"

They looked searchingly at one another, and Jon had an irresistible urge to look back at the doorway. There he saw an apparition of his own—or was it merely Anna returning to the room?

CHAPTER 13

▼

Rudi had excused himself at one o'clock because of an appointment, undisclosed to Violet for reasons known best to him. Moving hastily down Yelena's front steps, he hurried along Oscar's Gate and around two corners to the street where he had parked. Keyed up, trying to do everything faster than possible, he fumbled with the car lock and almost closed his fingers in the door. Sobered by these bungles, he made himself sit quietly while searching for at least a semblance of composure.

Even a semblance proved hard to come by, since he was about to engage in skullduggery on a scale hitherto unattempted by him. During and after the war he had entered into minor black market dealings, and more than once in his career he had lied to clients about the provenance of an art object or an appraisal. Such occasional lapses never involved more than a few thousand marks.

Risk generally increased in proportion to potential reward, Rudi knew, and by this standard his risk was due to increase about a thousand fold. Thanks to the immutable sequence of such things, he must face the risk before he gained the reward. Still, he told himself, the upcoming interview wouldn't risk everything. He was not necessarily staking his entire future on its outcome. All good risk takers have a backup plan, and he prided himself that he had one in the wings if things didn't work out.

This comforting thought calmed him sufficiently that he began worrying about his actual presentation—that is, about his ability to fool Felix Ratliff. Handling the novice Macleod was one thing; the formidable Ratliff was quite another. The prospect so unnerved him that only the fraud and larceny in his heart could spur him on.

Rudi carried an image of himself that he occasionally shared with others: the undiscovered Faberge of the late twentieth century. But for the replacement of Tsarist patronage by vulgar Communism, art experts would be praising him and wealthy aristocrats would be vying for his works. The pedestals now occupied by sports figures and rock stars would belong to him—to him to and artists of similar genius.

Rudi was, in fact, an excellent goldsmith and designer. What he lacked was happiness. He was not happy with the state of the world or with his place in it. He often lamented to Xenia that he had been born in the wrong century—that he would have been famous if he had lived in an age when working with gold and precious stones was as revered as painting and sculpture. He realized there was a certain childishness about his disappointment at not achieving fame, but attaching a label to a feeling did not make the feeling any less powerful. He knew that a man of sixty-four should display some degree of detachment, but the bitterness in his heart left no room for such accommodation.

Rudi admitted readily that he lacked objectivity when it came to his own work. Still, he did not look at his productions in relation to, say, the solar system. He took the narrower view of their superiority to most other contemporary efforts. Even so, this view had led to discontent, stress, and finally forgery.

He had expected an inheritance from Yelena for years, and in preparation for that happy day, he fashioned several objects. At night while Xenia slept or weekends when she visited friends, Rudi pulled his projects from their place of concealment and worked at them lovingly. There was of course never any need to hide his tools.

In this manner, over the years he had created three counterfeit Imperial Eggs with the intent of "discovering" them among Yelena's possessions following her death. This plan would give him a double satisfaction. His work would at last be recognized, albeit as another's, and he would cheat the shallow society that had scorned his artistry. Almost needless to say, he also anticipated millions of dollars.

Blending the genuine Faberge Eggs with those of his own making was the centerpiece of his plan. People, even knowledgeable people, would be much less inclined to question the provenance of Eggs "found" in Yelena's collection. Furthermore, uncertainty had always existed as to how many Eggs she possessed. From almost the beginning of her exile, rumors circulated of Yelena having all or most of the missing ones. As the years passed, Rudi promoted this supposition at every opportunity. Frequently he heard his own stories, sometimes embellished, from the lips of others.

Yelena's actual death brought unanticipated complications. In the first place, Rudi had failed to allow for the naming of Violet Strasser as his co-heir. In the second, even though Xenia and he searched desperately prior to Violet's arrival—not to say, ever since—they had yet to unearth the genuine Faberge Eggs.

Lacking the real Eggs, he nonetheless provided Macleod—and implicitly Felix Ratliff—with a plausible scenario. He pretended to have secured the treasured Imperial Eggs before Violet reached Oslo, so hopefully discouraging the Americans from contacting her. Even if this invention failed to prevent communication, it prepared Macleod and Ratliff for hearing Violet say the Eggs remained missing.

All well enough, except that Rudi, ill-advisedly, had specified the number of Eggs as six to Macleod, whereas only three could be currently produced. Those three were, of course, his own. Moreover, the number included none matching the description of Eggs widely known to be in Yelena's possession: the Egg of jade, the one of birch, and the Alexander III Commemorative Egg. To be unable to bring forth any of these three would immediately arouse Ratliff's skepticism.

Thus far Rudi had stalled successfully, both when Macleod came to Helsinki and yesterday over the telephone. But now came the summons to meet with Ratliff and possibly a much sterner test. There might be awkward questions and skillfully laid traps. He must manage the questions and avoid the traps, if the plan over which he had so long labored was to survive the afternoon.

Thus Rudi was much concerned as he drove the short distance to the Munch museum near the botanical gardens. Felix Ratliff had designated this location, and while some might question an art museum as a place to conduct unsavory business, Rudi knew the industrialist's need to kill two birds with one stone determined the selection. It was but another example of the grand executives of the twentieth century mixing business with their pleasure and vice versa.

Rudi was familiar with the Munch museum: low-lying and uninspired in the style of postwar park shelters. He was of course also familiar with the art of Edvard Munch, for whom he felt a certain limited goodwill, as one artist to another. Beyond that, as one Northern European to another, he accepted the climatic origins of Munch's "scream of nature." However, Rudi objected to Munch's modern idiom: the introverted sensitivity, the vague anxiety, the internalized passions. Rudi preferred grandeur.

"He's the Freud of painters," Felix Ratliff declared, not many minutes after they had met inside the museum, as they stood with Wally Macleod in front of *The Vampire*. Felix's words hung in the air like a Judgment Day fanfare. One half-expected a clap of thunder, or at least a ripple of applause.

All looked at *The Vampire*, until Felix began moving on to the next display. He had reached his seventies, but like many another wealthy man or woman, he looked much younger. He enjoyed a full head of hair—possibly his own—with no more gray than dark brown. An even tan—or was it bronze gel?—conveyed physical vigor. A beautifully tailored suit and professionally manicured hands dispelled any thought of incipient seediness.

"Now this," he singled out, stationing himself in front of a woodcut, "I like this." He stood back from the work and, folding one arm in support of the other, lightly feeling his smoothly shaven jaw.

Rudi stared. Since introductions by Wally, the conversation had amounted to a monologue as they toured the museum. Felix seemed to be establishing his mastery of Munch and his fellow Expressionists. He cited names and concepts as if on the way to passing his orals.

But now, suddenly, he interrupted erudition to advise, "I can spend only two more days here. I'll need to see your items by Tuesday, if it's to be this trip." He barely glanced at Rudi.

"I…I'll see what I can do."

"Wally says you have six." He moved to the next picture. "Is the 1917 companion among them?"

"I don't think so."

Wally broke in with, "That's turned up in Switzerland."

"Maybe," Felix demurred, stabbing each man briefly with his eyes.

"I've seen photographs," Rudi volunteered. "It looks more pat than it should."

"Ah." Felix favored him with a keen stare before returning his attention to the Munch in front of them. About that he commented, "You can see the influence of van Gogh prominently here." He used the Dutch pronunciation.

Rudi decided he could switch subjects every bit as well as Felix Ratliff. After all, changing subjects is considerably easier than changing languages, at which Rudi was adept. So he passed over the reference to van Gogh as van Gogh was passed over in life and asked instead how many Eggs had come into Ratliff's possession over the years.

Felix replied, "About fifteen. I've kept none."

"Have you seen the Kremlin's collection?"

"Yes."

"Which do you like best?" Rudi asked hastily, so postponing a dissertation on the next Munch exhibit.

"Of the Kremlin's?"

"Of all you've seen."

"I have no favorite. See here." He pointed to a greenish face. "The decay, the morbidity. Isn't it marvelous! And just think how early Munch came on!" He turned to Rudi. "Your wife's Russian, I believe?"

"Uh, yes."

"From Smolensk or thereabouts?"

"She lived there, but her family came from Vyatka."

"Vyatka?"

"It's called Kirov now."

"Of course, Kirov! Toward the Urals," and Felix took a step away, to begin examining the next painting. "See how the lines of hysteria converge! Tremendous, isn't it."

Rudi did not at all care for the reference to hysteria, because the dialogue about Xenia's origins had filled him with unease. Why would Felix Ratliff know anything about Xenia? Why would he care where she came from? And pretending not to know Vyatka except as "Kirov," named for that awful Communist dolt! After the Revolution they had gone about the country renaming everything! Nizhni Novgorod became "Gorki," Tsaritsyn, "Stalingrad," Ekaterinburg, "Sverdlovsk." All rechristened for dolts.

"…sharp lady, if she's anything like her father. What does she say about it?" Felix was asking him.

"I beg your pardon? I was thinking about the painting."

Again Felix bent upon Rudi that cold, knifelike glance, so peculiarly at odds with the benignly set lines of his visage, with the delicately civilized trappings of his person. "Violet Strasser," he said. "How are you putting her off?" He lightly stressed "her."

"We're all hunting for the Eggs," Rudi replied simply.

"Ah, I see. I understand there's a relative of some sort with her?"

"Xenia and I are Violet's cousins."

"Somebody else."

"You mean Jon Olsen? We're also cousins to him. He arrived yesterday."

Now Wally spoke. "How long will he stay?"

"A few days. I think he's leaving Thursday." Then Rudi added with a degree of ingenuousness, "Did you meet him on the ship?"

"I made a point of it."

"What did you think of him?"

Felix cut in with, "It doesn't matter what Wally thinks." Ignoring Wally's look of displeasure, Ratliff addressed Rudi. "What do *you* think?"

Rudi answered carefully, "I'll be glad when he's gone. He's a potential danger."

Rudi saw Wally start to say something, but Felix held up a silencing finger and led the way into the next gallery. Behind his back, Rudi and Wally exchanged a questioning look.

Felix now resumed the intermittent discourse on Edvard Munch with a supplemental lecture on woodcuts. He instructed with his back to the others, who were thus emboldened to engage in meaningful grimaces. Wally formed the words "Eleven tonight" with his lips, and Rudi nodded in understanding.

Shortly afterwards, Felix wheeled around, without however catching the others in their communications. He said to Rudi, "Maybe you prefer to wait until this person is gone."

Rudi had to recollect which person he meant before answering, "Oh yes. I'd very much prefer when Jon's gone." It gave him, after all, more time.

"I can rearrange my schedule: leave tomorrow and come back Thursday. Wally will let you know." He began moving from the gallery, evidently with the intention of leaving the museum altogether, although they had not inspected all the collection.

In Felix's wake, Wally leaned toward Rudi and whispered, "The Concert Hall," then pulled ahead, to keep up with his employer. Finding himself near a snack area, Rudi hesitated, for he had taken no lunch. There were numerous student types loitering about displaying beards and backpacks, dilated pupils and thick glasses. Rudi elected to head outdoors.

He came outside in time to see the others pulling away in a sedan. They had a driver. The car took off with a puff of smoke from its exhaust. The smoke swirled briefly and then dissipated, so recalling a performance of "Faust" that Rudi had once seen. Only this Mephistopheles was exiting in a Mercedes Benz.

By the time Rudi reached his own car, he was worried again. How could there be any assurance Yelena's Eggs would be found by Thursday? And what real chance was there of keeping the full price for himself, anyway? How could he possibly keep from sharing the profits with Violet? He knew he couldn't bear to split income from his own work with another. And after the encounter today, it was hard for him to consider Wally Macleod a serious buyer. He doubted Wally could pay more than Felix Ratliff for even one Egg.

The fact was that all those exhausting nights, all those grandiose dreams might be for nothing or—almost worse—for fifty percent.

He wanted to weep.

CHAPTER 14

▼

Jon showered, shaved, and dressed meticulously for his dinner date with Georgia Beech. He selected a white button-down shirt with gray pinstripes and a pearl gray sports jacket. He cleaned his nails and shined his shoes. As a result of all this effort, he looked almost impressive, he admitted, studying himself in the mirror. Perhaps he could even be considered handsome in a rather large, alarming way.

Although he gauged his effect accurately, he felt little satisfaction because his conscience bothered him. There was no reason for this—no real reason at all. He understood that, too, without ceasing to be troubled.

The thing had to do with Anna, who had worked religiously on Yelena's books and correspondence during the late afternoon, right down to evening, when Violet closed up the house and the three of them parted. Anna had said goodbye so modestly, had extended her hand so tentatively, had lifted her head so bravely that he—well, damn it! The fact that he owed her no explanations whatsoever made things worse, rather than better!

Why the devil had he begun feeling obligated to her? All his life he had been scrupulous in observing the Marquees of Queensbury rules as they applied to flirtation and courtship: no wrestling and no slugging in the clinches. Furthermore, he had never misled any woman, nor would. And if that was the secret to his bachelor-dom, so be it.

But now, with Anna, the rules—or maybe the entire sport—had changed. It had to do with her obsession, with her making a fetish of him. He was being made to feel that he played unfairly, that he cheated or something, that his standards were inadequate for the task at hand. If he didn't watch out, it would spoil even this evening with Georgia!

He looked again at himself in the mirror and saw a brow furrowed with uncertainty. This would simply never do! He wanted very much to see Georgia, to be with Georgia. It was folly to meet a woman like that with trouble in his heart. She'd sense it right away and be amused at his expense. She'd view him as an insipid adolescent. Well, he wouldn't have it!

Resolutely, he moved his shoulders inside the pearl gray jacket and set out for Georgia's nearby hotel. He subdued his not-quite-guilty conscience with the thought of Georgia's laugh, Georgia's eyes, and Georgia's body. More than merely effective, this cure stimulated an incredible number of brain synapses, none of them leading to an image of Anna Nygaard.

At the hotel, Georgia and her friends waited in the lobby. Jon, in the best international style, embraced Georgia lightly while bestowing a dispassionate kiss on her cheek, although every fiber of his being demanded more. Were his manner to be faulted at all, it would be for an almost infinitesimal delay in releasing her.

She introduced him to Peter and Deborah Van Cleef, and then they all moved into the main dining room, where the maitre d' led them to a satisfactory table. Jon followed immediately behind Georgia, who was probably the most sumptuously packaged life force this particular dining room was ever likely to see.

As the maitre d' seated her, her ringlets bobbed delightfully and her ample bosom heaved in a contented sigh. Jon noted the awe on the maitre d's face, nor was it unlike his own sentiment at the moment. With an act of will, he turned his eyes from her to Deborah Van Cleef.

"Are you of the Michigan Olsens?" Mrs. Van Cleef asked, in that way Southern women often have of zeroing in on family. "My daddy knew an Eric Olsen in Ann Arbor, possibly one of your relations?"

"It's possible we're related, being from the same part of the country, but I've never paid much attention to the family genealogy. As far as I know, most of my family is from Minnesota." When she looked somewhat disappointed, he continued, "What was your father's name?"

"Harwick Randolph."

"I'd certainly remember, if I'd heard it."

"But you don't?"

"Sorry, can't say that I do. Where did your father live?"

"Kentucky. We all live in Kentucky. Is there anywhere else?" she asked playfully, with a toss of her thin hands that caused the large diamond solitaire to flash coldly, brilliantly. Then she leaned toward Georgia, seated on the opposite side of the table, and added, "Georgia's still a Texan at heart, but we forgive her."

Too quickly, Jon looked at the subject of this remark, and his heart actually skipped a beat. She simply overwhelmed his senses, including good sense. He just looked at her, kept looking at her, while she smiled at him.

Deborah Van Cleef finally quipped, "Why Georgia, I think he's smitten."

Georgia smiled. "Don't be silly, Deb."

"You're smitten, aren't you, Olsen?"

Jon broke off his gazing at the delicious Georgia to bring his blue-gray eyes to bear on Deborah. "Of course," he said, his face impassive.

"Good man," Peter interjected. "We all love Georgia." It sounded as if he meant it, but in a fraternal, conceptual way—that is to say, not Jon's way. "What's your particular line?"

"You mean, what do I do?" and Jon mentioned his profession.

"How interesting. I've never known a civil engineer before. However, I'll not ask for details, since I would doubtless have trouble understanding them." He was a tall man, of slight build, with a rolling Southern accent and tanned face. His hands, beautifully shaped, were probably very strong.

The Van Cleefs bred and raced horses. A great grandfather had started the family on its way with dry goods and groceries, parlayed later into a chain store operation. Deborah's father had married into one of the great Virginia families, and Deborah, into Kentucky bourbon via Peter.

Jon learned these facts during dinner, since the Van Cleefs proved to be accomplished conversationalists. They told their tales in tandem: Deborah sketched the story line and set the pace, while Peter interpolated with dry commentaries and absurd details. The result came close to high comedy, and Jon could not but be entertained despite constant awareness of Georgia on his left.

He sensed she was looking at him whenever he spoke and even, from time to time, when he listened. He wondered whether it might be the scar she examined, but he dare not again look her way too suddenly. Rather, he planned each time his eyes turned upon her, so bracing himself beforehand. It seemed the prudent thing to do.

Yet always, when his eyes encountered hers, he felt a small, silent rush of adrenaline, not forceful enough to make him draw in his breath, but identifiable nonetheless. That a sensation of this kind existed at all under such decorous circumstances rather boggled his mind. Certainly he couldn't spend many meals in this condition without risking ulcers, misconduct, or worse.

Georgia returned his glances—for they seldom lasted longer than that—with unnerving serenity. It was as if she knew all his secrets: his courage and size, his loneliness and uncertainty, his fastidiousness and lust. She had Mona Lisa's air of seeing all without judging, of smiling without mercy, of keeping wisdom to herself.

Yet he managed to carry on his part of the conversation, to speak of Carolina Barnwells and Old Dominion Masons, of Seabiscuit and Native Dancer, of tennis shots and deep sea catches. And Deborah did not again accuse him of being smitten nor failing in attention any other way. Indeed, upon parting after dinner in the lobby, the Van Cleefs pronounced him "delightful," at which Georgia turned to view Jon's reaction.

He was gazing after Peter and Deborah, as they made their way to the elevators. There was no expression on his face.

"Did you like them?" she asked.

"Yes." He looked at her quickly, then past her shoulder.

"Well, are we going to take that walk?"

"If you like."

"I don't like unless you do."

"I suggested it," he stated, more or less as a correction. Now he steeled himself to look at her steadily, to find the actual process not so difficult after all. "Let's go." He took her by the arm and steered toward the revolving door.

The air caught her lively ringlets and bore the swishing sound of her skirts, not to say the incense of her perfume. As they passed through the doors, he briefly guided her with his hand upon her hip, so that he asked, "Do you have this effect on every man you meet?"

"What effect?"

"The one you're having on me."

"Maybe I don't understand the effect I'm having," she replied, with a certain mindful gravity. They were outside now and soon left the marquee and overhead light behind them. Until their eyes adjusted to the darkness, neither could see the other's features.

He wanted very much to grab her and make love to her on the spot, but such behavior was naturally out of the question. He said, "Deborah didn't mistake the effect you're having."

She did not answer at once. He could hear her heels clicking on the sidewalk, could see her shape and the ghostly oval of he face. Finally she said, "'Smitten,' do you mean? I don't count that real likely."

"Only being smitten could make me confess to it. Nothing else. Not social justice nor red-hot pincers."

Her pleasant laugh drifted on the night's air and gladdened his unsure heart, right up until she next spoke: "Have you told that to your answering service?"

"My what?"

"The woman who answers your phone."

Damn! She meant Anna! "Oh, that," he said lamely. "I can explain."

"By all means," she invited, sounding amused.

"It's a girl from the Embassy. She's helping with my aunt's affairs."

"The estate, you mean."

"Yes, the estate. Look here." He stopped, causing her to pause as well, "It's a ridiculous matter."

"I believe you," and she laughed again, but without gladdening his heart.

"What do you believe?"

"That she's from the Embassy and working on the estate. That it's a ridiculous matter."

He gave a guttural sigh of frustration. Then he said, "Forgive me, but both of us can be misunderstood. I'd never ask you to explain Felix Ratliff."

She looked startled, but not for long. "You're very clever."

"No. No, I'm almost out of control."

"Well now, I can't buy that," she declared.

"Maybe you should."

They were standing some distance from a lamppost set inside the park they were skirting. The light was such that her features appeared as approximations of themselves, that edges diffused like ink on wet paper. Only as they moved in relation to the lamp did her shadowed eyes sometimes gleam with borrowed sparks.

She took a step backward by which she would have been out of most men's reach, but not Jon's. "I guess maybe I didn't understand," she said, sounding very straight-shooting, very Southwestern.

"And now that you do?"

"I could lie to you."

"I wouldn't want that."

"You wouldn't know," she advised him, her voice matter-of-fact.

He shoved his hands in his pockets. "Why lie?"

"A girl has to protect herself."

Feeling encouraged, he said, "Okay, tell me your lie."

As she turned a little, her eyes caught the light momentarily and flashed it phosphorescently into the night. At the same time, she hugged herself, as if in defense from chill. "It's time to call it a night," she stated in tones as flat and unyielding as any plain in Texas.

"Is that your lie?"

"No, it's not."

"Well, you warned me I wouldn't know," he conceded. He blocked the way to the hotel completely now. If she chose to walk away from him, it must be into the park.

Perhaps partly in recognition of her strategic disadvantage, she spoke more directly. "I'm married. And I don't cheat."

"Yet you called me."

"Wally Macleod asked me to."

He caught his breath. "What!" His hands inside the pockets clenched into fists as a surge of anger and alarm temporarily obliterated his customary good sense. Faster than the eye could follow, his right hand shot out and seized her wrist. "Why did he want you to call me?"

"Hey, you don't know your own strength!" She did not sound frightened.

"*Why!*" He had both wrists now.

"Well, gee! I don't know. Maybe he's out right now with that woman who answers your phone."

He had pulled her right up to him and only after the fact realized how this closeness determined everything that followed: his laugh, her smile, his release of her wrists to recapture all of her in his arms. He kissed her. She was resistant at first, then compliant, then resistant again. "I won't let you go," he growled.

"You must! Jon, you must!"

"That's your lie," he guessed. He began kissing her again, her hair, her temple, her cheek.

"No! It's not!"

He tried to kiss her neck, and she pulled away. "Don't worry, this is a public place. Come here."

She shook her head.

"Come here."

And when she acquiesced, when she stopped resisting him, when she in fact responded to his passion, a vast contentment engulfed him, and he felt he could die happy now.

But only now, this moment, with Georgia Beech in his arms.

C H A P T E R   15

▼

Xenia's mother was an orphan, one of the multitudes spawned in the deadly course of the Russian Revolution. Her documented life began at approximately six years old, when she was found, cold and hungry, begging on the streets of Vyatka, since named Kirov. It was the year 1925, and Lenin was already dead.

She was dressed in rags and—much more remarkably—wore a gold chain about her neck. This chain probably would have caused her trouble with the authorities, had she not exchanged it the first night in Vyatka for bread. The peasant who sold her the bread called himself Mitkin and declared he was doing her a favor.

She knew her own name as "Stasia," and when asked where she came from, pointed toward the setting sun. However, there was little reason to suppose she originally came from anywhere in particular. She had no inkling as to where the events of her short life had occurred, including her birth.

This dismal, incomplete beginning does not at all convey the complexity of Stasia's early memories, much later imparted to others, at least those details she salvaged from oblivion. Her recollections included mountains and woods and wolves, photographs of elegant ladies with ostrich-plumed hats, a tray of gemstones, a pile of putrefying bodies, and an ugly man with an ax. These images followed no orderly sequence of any kind.

It was not until adolescence that Stasia imposed meaning on the rich and disturbing hodgepodge of childhood remnants. Her invented order imitated the folk tales of nobility in disguise and may also have reflected logic lost in her subconscious. In any case, from the flotsam and jetsam of her early life she fashioned a story of romance and tragedy that incidentally conferred royalty upon herself.

Her story went like this: When the Bolsheviks massacred the last Tsar and his family, a guard spared and then hid Tatiana, the second and most fashionable of the Tsar's four daughters. In due course, Tatiana and her proletarian protector became lovers, with Stasia the ultimate result. Tatiana named the baby after her deceased sister Anastasia, before dying herself from complications following the birth. The father cared for Stasia until his defection from Socialist morality was detected, whereupon he was taken away and shot.

Stasia based her father's fate on a single memory: he left one morning in the company of soldiers, and later in the day a man gave her a pair of boots, allegedly her father's. That was all. She never saw him again, nor could she remember much else about him except that he kept her mother's pictures near the ikons and once brought Stasia three oranges. Nevertheless, she believed her story completely.

When she herself gave birth for the first time, Stasia named her daughter "Xenia," despite mild objections from her cautious husband. Either from her Socialist education or from oral tradition, Stasia knew of the royal connection, of Grand Duchess Xenia Alexandrovna, and of the last Tsar's niece Xenia Georgievna. She chose this "family" name over that of the universally unpopular last Empress'.

By the time Xenia was six, the family was fleeing Russia, possibly in part because Stasia had shared the imagined circumstances of her own descent with all her husband's immediate relatives, so leading to official notice of an unwelcome sort. Dying in an Austrian camp for displaced persons, Stasia was buried fairly unceremoniously near Graz. Although her death proved the end of her, it did not end the legend of her origins.

Had Stasia lived, her story of Romanov ancestry might have died in Xenia from good sense. Stasia possessed an extremely narrow education and many peasant ways, so that Xenia—so clever by nature and so fashionable by inherited good taste—might soon have rejected her mother's tale as the general fiction it was. But with the mother dead and her memory sentimentalized by a slightly conscience-stricken father, Xenia grew up to believe all she'd heard. Nothing solid interfered with wanting to believe, with wanting to be the last Tsar's great granddaughter.

Xenia did not talk about it, any more than she discussed her good looks or money-mindedness. Of course, the latter characteristics could be seen or inferred by others, whereas royalty could not. Yet she treated the three as equally factual.

She only once touched on the topic with Rudi, who, in the course of courtship, heard certain gossip. "Yes," Xenia told him in her business-like way, "Grandmere was an aristocrat, probably Romanov. Only who can zay?" Her shrug was Gallic. "What are Communist records?" Typically, Rudi took this at face value and asked no further questions, so foreshadowing the shallow exchanges that passed for communication in their later married life.

Yet each was secretive and deep, if in very different ways. Xenia hugged all sorts of secrets: the Romanov legend, a nest egg gathered cautiously from the shop's earnings, a desire to live in Paris—all sorts of secrets. Just a few weeks ago, she had learned one of Rudi's secrets. She had found his fake "Faberge eggs."

As soon as she saw the eggs, nestled in an old tool case opened merely because it seemed oddly placed, she grasped both their pretension and Rudi's intention. Marveling, she lifted them from their hiding place one by one: a silver egg with snowflakes engraved, and inside, a troika; an egg cared from malachite; and the masterpiece, an egg-shaped cage of gold encasing a bejeweled, enameled lilac bush in full bloom, so exquisite Xenia caught her breath.

To think these were Rudi's work! And to think what he planned! She returned the lilac Egg to the case and slowly seated herself at the workbench. Leaving the lid open, she contemplated what Rudi had wrought and his probable scheme of things.

An official letter had informed him of his co-inheritance from Yelena a fortnight before. Xenia had felt surprise at their not setting out for Oslo at once, but now she saw the delay's probable cause. Rudi had to finish the last—whichever it was—of the eggs before making the journey, in order to "find" it among Yelena's things. How very ingenious of him!

She kept her knowledge from him, not merely out of habit. The next few days she watched him unobtrusively, while spending many thoughts on her discovery. Romanov thoughts came to dominate. She dwelled increasingly on the real Imperial Eggs as property, as *her* property—not Rudi's or Violet Strasser's.

She determined her objective and plotted to this end: living well in Paris as the last Tsar's last descendent. She observed Rudi's actions, thereby learning where he stashed the fake eggs for their trip to Norway. She also guessed that Wally Macleod, that seemingly casual American visitor to their shop, carried out a mission. "We have a cousin on ze *Queen Anne*," she had said, and Mr. Macleod did not look surprised to hear it.

After Rudi and she reached Oslo, after they gained access to Yelena's house, Xenia easily convinced him he should do the cataloguing while she surveyed the correspondence. And she was lucky. The day before Violet arrived, she found Yelena's letters revealing where the Imperial Eggs lay hidden. With an inadvertent, furtive look, she folded the letters, from someone named Vaino, and put them in the pocket of her skirt. Even though Rudi worked diligently up front, even though he could have no suspicion of her theft, she covered the outside of the pocket with her hand, as if further shielding her prize from discovery.

That evening at their lodging, while Rudi bathed, Xenia took the letters into the garden and burned them on a stone. With her spike heels, she pulverized any remaining bits of scorched paper and then pushed and blew the ashes into the dirt. Thus she achieved the satisfaction of knowing no one was likely ever again to see Yelena's fabled Imperial Eggs without a Romanov's help.

The next day she felt no compulsion to act, but rather reviewed the situation. Because the Eggs' location posed a physical obstacle for her, she required an ally. But who? She pondered the question several days and meanwhile Jon Olsen showed up. She flirted with him and read his palm and did not immediately make up her mind even though he *did* look like Jean Sibelius. But then, during their outing on Bygdøy, in the Viking ship museum, she saw him looking from one resurrected vessel to an artifact in the case beside him, and she perceived—with an alarm that made her stumble—how he or someone else might put the puzzle together even without the letters as guide.

*   *   *   *

Once parted from Anna and Jon at the pier below the Radhuset, Xenia took not a step toward Yelena's, for she had no intention of returning that day. On the assumption Rudi was quietly cataloguing in Oscars Gate, she headed for their lodgings with the purpose of opening a bottle of wine and sitting in the garden while devising a final plan of action. How displeased she was to find Rudi already there, and with a bottle of wine as well!

"What are you doing here?" she asked accusingly in German. Generally they spoke German or French, the languages in which they made the least number of mistakes.

"I might ask you the same," he replied.

She studied him a moment. "You look worried."

"Take no notice."

"Very well, then." She sat down opposite him, while putting her bottle and glass on the table. She poured her wine and drank before volunteering, "We had a splendid walk."

"Did you find out anything?"

"No. The beautiful American woman made our cousin mad. But then, I think that's her technique."

"How, 'technique'?"

"For catching him."

Rudi stayed silent for a moment, then asked, "Why does she want to catch him?"

"You can ask that? Do you see nothing?" When he did not reply, she continued, "Where did you go from Yelena's? Or have you been here all afternoon?"

He took a sip of wine before answering, "I dropped by the Munch museum."

"That morbid place?"

"It's not without interest."

"Everyone to his taste," she conceded, this time in French.

"So. I don't especially like Munch," he acknowledged, without going into why.

Evidently Xenia did not care, for she now exclaimed, "What a beautiful afternoon!"

That ended the conversation. Rudi looked out toward the garden and drank. Xenia picked up her bottle, her glass, and herself and proceeded to walk about the paths, just as if she had not already been to Bygdøy and back by foot. In due course, she wandered into the house, leaving him to his thoughts.

*   *   *   *

Later on that evening, Rudi and Xenia joined Violet for dinner at the hotel. Violet seemed keyed up, saying she was "onto something." Xenia disguised her anxiety at this remark and waited for Rudi to inquire into the matter. When Violet thereupon launched into a description of her nephew's search plan, Xenia relaxed. It was nothing.

"Where's Jon tonight?" she asked.

Making an impatient movement with her hand, Violet rolled her big, black eyes. "With someone named Georgia."

"Not someone you know?"

"Good Heavens no! I've never met her."

"An American?"

"Oh, I imagine," replied Violet. Then she added with an air of mystification, "It's very odd, but until the last few days I've never thought of Jon as, well, frivolous."

"Frivolous?" inquired Rudi.

"Trifling with women, you know, attractive to them. Oh, he's handsome enough, but a woman—even a predatory one—needs encouragement. And he just doesn't give them any. He's a born bachelor, as anyone can see. Except Anna doesn't seem to see."

"Oh," said Xenia, "As for zat…" and she shrugged.

"What do you mean?"

"Xenia says Anna's after our cousin," Rudi offered.

"Oh, she is! She definitely is!" agreed Violet. "A person couldn't be more determined about something less consequential!"

"You think Jon's inconsequential?"

"No, certainly not! I mean, Jon's impervious, and determination can do her no good." Looking from one to the other, Violet seemed to be soliciting their corroboration.

"No one's impervious," Rudi told her.

And Xenia said, "Jon has a serious weakness. He's a gentleman."

"Oh, but that's just superficial. That exterior veneer covers solid oak. His mother was that way: stubborn beyond belief."

"What do you mean, darlink?"

"They get something in their minds, and nothing changes it," Violet explained. "Like tonight. Nothing Anna could say changed his determination."

"What determination?"

"To go out with this Georgia person."

"Maybe he's just escaping from Anna," suggested Rudi, with a smile.

"No. He was bound to see her. I could tell: nothing, literally nothing, could stop him. Not tears, not bribes, not earthquakes, not heart attacks. Just like his mother!"

"You don't mean to say Anna cried?" asked Xenia.

"Oh, no!"

The three of them sat there, contemplating Violet's thesis and the vision of Anna, trying to stop Jon without tears.

Then Xenia murmured, "I wonder who zis Georgia is."

Widening her eyes, Violet answered, "Anna says she came to Oslo with Felix Ratliff. Did you know he's here?"

Rudi upset his wine goblet, and Xenia stared wonderingly at each of her companions in turn, as her husband apologized profusely for his awkwardness and Violet sopped up wine with the extra napkin.

"He's in Oslo?" asked Xenia.

"Yes. A world class vulture, you understand." Violet looked at the waiter as she turned the clean-up job over to him.

"Er, why do you suppose Jon is dealing with friends of Ratliff?" inquired Rudi.

"You make it sound faintly sinister."

"I merely asked."

"I don't think he's 'dealing' at all," Violet advised. "He's just being stubborn about this woman."

Xenia noted how Rudi chewed his lip, how he lowered his head and looked at Violet from under his graying eyebrows. He seemed afraid to ask more, but also dying to do so. Meanwhile Violet, fussing with her helping of surstek, gave the appearance of total divorcement from the topic of Felix Ratliff.

Rudi finally ventured to inquire how stubbornness explained Jon's initial impulse to ask a lady out. He put the matter most delicately, so as not to offend Cousin Violet. He took care not to imply too strongly that her original presentation was in any way deficient, but he did put it.

Violet looked up from poking her surstek. "Are you accusing my nephew of disloyalty?" she demanded, the well-known Strasser family pride coming to the fore and steam rolling all other considerations. "Because I never heard anything so ridiculous!"

"I didn't mean...."

"Yes you did!"

"Now Violet!"

"I *told* you he's being frivolous! *That's* the problem! He's for some reason suddenly in demand—at least, I think it's suddenly."

They sat in silence for a moment, watching Violet struggle with her surstek. Xenia could almost feel Rudi's anxiety to probe further, but he said nothing.

Suddenly Violet added, "This Georgia person, too! Anna told me all about it, how this woman called Jon and how he's—I think she said—'bonkers' over her. That means sappy, I take it." And although at the end of this communication she still sounded feisty, she had begun to look a little unsure.

Xenia put out her hand to touch Violet's sleeve. "I don't for a minute zink Jon's anyzink but honorable, so naturally women like him."

"Yes, of course. But only to escort them places."

"Yes, zat too," agreed Xenia.

This may have been the conversation that made up Xenia's mind. She wondered if perhaps it made up Violet's too.

CHAPTER 16

▼

Jon awoke to a persistent rapping at his door. He called out, "Just a minute!," and rolled out of bed. Grabbing a pair of shorts, he pulled these on and opened the blinds to let in a little sun. His watch showed 6:45.

After shaking sleep from his eyes and pushing back the hair from his forehead, he opened the door to discover it was Anna. She stood there, smartly dressed in navy and white, a leather handbag draped from her shoulder, every blonde hair in place. "May I come in?"

As he gave way and the door swung toward the wall, she sailed inside. She went directly to the bed he had just vacated and, after throwing the spread to cover the sheets, sat down. "Tell me how it all went last night," she urged, as if they were dormitory girls eager to discuss last night's dates.

"Uh, if you don't mind, I'll just put on a shirt," he proposed, and picked up several items on his way to the bathroom.

"Will you be long? I mean, I have to go to work."

He just gave her a cool stare and closed the door behind him.

She waited until the toilet flushed and he was brushing his teeth before calling, "Don't bother to shave. I haven't time."

The door opened. "What's that?" he asked, through toothpaste.

"I said, don't bother to shave."

He kicked the door shut.

In a few minutes, he came out, unshaven, wearing a tennis shirt and shorts. He was still barefoot. "All right. To what do I owe such an early morning call?"

"My work."

"Anna," he said warningly.

"Tell me all about it. Where you went, what you did."

"We went to dinner. We talked."

"If that's all, it must have been very disappointing."

"I wouldn't say that."

"Did you bring her here?"

He watched her a moment before countering, "Aren't you afraid you'll be late for work?"

"I'm never afraid. Did you bring her here?"

Answering nothing, he gazed at her steadily.

"Well, it really doesn't matter, I suppose. You brought *me* here and nothing happened." She cocked her head so that her hair fell in silky undulations, eyeing him critically.

He ran a hand over his face in a gesture of impatience and futility, then said mildly, "Anna, I don't want to talk about it."

"About Georgia Beech?"

"I don't want to talk about it."

"Because you're not really awake?"

"I'm awake."

"I'd think you'd want to talk about it. And it's extremely important to me."

"There's no reason for it to be," he stated, purposefully putting an edge to his voice, as he folded his arms across his chest.

"No reason? You must be crazy! That woman's my rival!"

"She's—I don't want to talk about it."

"You keep saying that."

"Exactly."

They looked at one another a number of seconds as antagonists. Then, favoring him with a lukewarm smile, she announced, "I'll go ask *her.*" She juggled her shoulder bag preparatory to getting up.

He started toward her at once, glowering, and, bending over, took her by the shoulders. "I forbid it!" he exclaimed.

"Oh, Jon! You're magnificent when you're mad!"

"Are you listening?"

"You're so masterful!"

"Listen to me!" he commanded, sitting on the bed beside her and shaking her a bit. He forced a quiet menace into his voice. "I forbid it!"

"But you can't. Not really," she replied intrepidly.

"If you defy me in this, you lose me. Absolutely."

"Ah!" she breathed. "I see."

He released her and buried his face in his hands. As it so happened, the label of his shirt was sticking above the collar, and Anna fussed and patted it into place. This act seemed naturally to lead to massaging his neck and shoulders, whereupon he raised his head and turned his face away.

"I don't want to lose you," she said, a rare softness to her voice.

"You don't even know me," came his muttered reply.

"I've known you two days."

He did not respond.

"Okay," she said cheerfully. "I'll look on the bright side. I'll take your words to mean I haven't lost you yet."

He shifted restlessly, still not letting her see his face.

She trailed her fingers along his neck to the edge of his jaw "Whatever happened last night, I still have a chance." Trying to see some part of his face, she twisted forward a little.

Abruptly he removed her hand from his neck and faced her, while putting more distance between them. He struggled to appear totally impassive. "We must come to an understanding," he said.

"Oh, certainly."

"I'm at least fifteen years older than you. I'm independent and won't be told how to live my life...by anybody. I live in Minnesota, and when I go abroad, it's on vacation. I'm hardly a man of the world."

She continued to gaze earnestly at him. In due course she acknowledged, "Understood. Minnesota, is it? Well, maybe after we're married, I could run for public office."

One eyebrow arched as be replied, "You go too fast."

"It's my nature. It's me. That's why we're so perfect for one another. Don't you see? We balance, Jon. Why can't you admit that?"

"I want to hear your terms," he persisted.

"I'll do anything to get you!"

"That's irrelevant."

"No. It's true."

"Your terms."

"I haven't any."

"Describe yourself, then."

"I don't introspect," she told him.

He gave a groan of frustration, slapped his palm against his thighs and stood up. "You'll be late for work."

She rose, too, and flung her arms about his neck, the shoulder bag thumping his sides. "Jon, I love you! Can't you relate to that? Can't you see? I <u>love</u> you!"

Patiently, gently, he extricated himself, while answering, "My dear, I live by reason, and so I need reasons for all things, especially something this amazing."

They stepped apart, after which Anna regarded him scientifically and then announced, "I'm twenty-seven years old. My I.Q.'s a hundred and fifty-six. I don't have any of the popular social diseases. I know what you need, and I'm going to spell it out at tonight at 8:30." She was digging into her purse. "Here's my address." She handed him her card. "Eight thirty," she repeated and went out the door.

Dumbfounded, he stood with his back to her as she let herself out, her card in his hand. He stared at the object in disbelief, while a kind of numbness invaded his thought processes. Was he going mad?

Well, why not? Here he stood like a fool looking at a piece of paper, and she had gotten away unchallenged. In fact, the whole scene he'd just been through was unthinkable. He'd been hauled from his bed for a sorority sister chat about a woman driving him mad with passion, *with* a woman who drove him mad, period! Did sanity survive such things?

He made a motion to throw away the card, but then, after a moment's hesitation, reached for his wallet and placed the card carefully inside. How could he insult her by not showing up? The time to have said no was past, and he'd thereby obligated himself to another ridiculous experience! How he dreaded 8:30!

He sat on the windowsill and looked down at the street below, where Norwegians scurried to their jobs like something bigger than ants. Beetles, perhaps.

If only Aunt Violet hadn't summoned him to Oslo, then this entire muddle would never have been. His resolve at Helsingør would have held firm, and Anna Nygaard would not exist for him, nor he for her. At almost this very moment he could be disembarking from the *Queen Anne* in Amsterdam after enjoying an uninterrupted Baltic vacation. Instead of this evening's painful encounter, he could be flying back to Minnesota and those waiting designs for a new suburban rail system.

Except that, somehow, this silent scenario didn't quite ring true. What might have been didn't seem so very appealing, did it. Against all sense, anguish over Georgia and exasperation with Anna evidently suited him better, so tending to confirm a diagnosis of madness. Perversely, he seemed to be enjoying chaos and frustration. He felt unhappy but stimulated. He had almost said "alive."

But deep inside he knew the frenzy of lust, whether for a woman or power, only signified childlike indulgence of self. It was true that momentary pleasurable sensations, cloaked by the pretext of love or justice or the public good, could be addictive. But he asked himself if he truly wanted a daily fix of such frenzy.

No such hedonistic vistas had presented themselves at the start of his journey. He had been looking at how things worked and how people lived. The breakfasts and lunches with Mme. Perpignan, the Baltic islands and harbors, the old cities, the reports of Russian subs in Swedish waters—all had interested him without absorbing him, so permitting the exercise of his considerable powers of observation.

Was it in Leningrad the transformation began, the transformation from reason to irrationality? Had it started when he mounted the stairs of the Winter Palace, perhaps, and imagined himself an intruder swept up by the revolutionary mob? Or when, spotting Wally Macleod with the Soviet official, he had reacted like some celluloid spy?

Or was it on the drive to Helsingør, sepulcher of a dim kingdom's dimmer past, with the magically vital Georgia at his side? How else could he account for his expenditure of that day, for his recalling almost nothing about Helsingr and more than everything about Georgia?

And look at him now, sitting in an Oslo hotel window, barefoot, unshaven, and without breakfast—all details entirely out of character, out of order. And "introspecting," as Anna would say. He, Jon Olsen, introspecting! It defied common sense!

Common sense. Well, at least Georgia had it, retained it, whereas he…Well, was it possible, was it really possible he had fallen in love? At his age? Why, he barely knew her, no more than Anna knew him! Theirs were similarly absurd infatuations.

He could not fault Aunt Violet for chiding him on his dissipation of time promised for her affairs. What had he done for her except walk out to a Bygdøy museum and back? In Oslo two days, and he had accomplished nothing except tying one on and making goo-goo eyes at Georgia. No, nor even that, exactly.

He must get on with it, with Aunt Violet's affairs, beginning with the fact that neither Rudi nor Xenia came back to Yelena's yesterday afternoon. Conceivably that connected with something Georgia had mentioned about how Wally and Felix Ratliff were in Oslo on business. Might not their business be with the Andersons?

Aunt Violet was right to question their cousins' intentions. After all, Rudi and Xenia had showed up first in Oslo and had broken their long-standing date with Jon in Helsinki to do it. If they had found the Eggs already, might not they now be selling these to Ratliff?

Come to think of it, hadn't Xenia proposed and enthused over the outing to Bygdøy? Admittedly, she managed spectacularly in high heels, but was a walk that long likely to appeal even to her? So had she perhaps played decoy, while Rudi greased the skids for selling Aunt Violet's inheritance? Not a very pretty prospect, but clever—clever enough to make a dupe of Jon.

According to Georgia and the Van Cleefs, Ratliff flew from Oslo sometime today, but would return later in the week. What for? For completing his business? That might indicate a need to collect currency for a transaction already agreed upon. Because with Aunt Violet excluded from any deal, Ratliff would be forced to come up with millions in cash without leaving a money trail. And how did one do that?

It was then that Jon thought of the Soviet Union. Ratliff could go to the Communists for safe money. That might be the purpose of Wally's little meeting behind the Hermitage. The fact was, having sold off Imperial Eggs in earlier decades, the Soviets now wanted some of them back to preserve the pre-eminence of the Kremlin collection. It would look bad if the English—or, God forbid, the Americans!—had the pre-eminent collection of Imperial Russian Eggs.

Jon left his window perch to begin dressing. He was determined to meet with Aunt Violet at Yelena's at once. However much he yearned after Georgia, he must wait until this afternoon to see her again.

CHAPTER 17

▼

Where had life on the Texas plains gone, Georgia wondered—that straight-forward, scrub-oak existence, with cattle and a pickup truck and a movie in town Saturday nights? A place where she knew everybody, and everybody followed the code or moved on? A time when a little could please you a lot, and a lot didn't look like so very much? Why did it no longer exist and yet govern her still?

It sometimes seemed that where one happened to be at a particular moment in time wasn't the ideal place to be. It was then that one's past looked less complicated and much more appealing than the present. Like now, when she realized she had to flee Jon Olsen. Her past was catching up with her—overtaking her, even possessing her.

Of course, one could argue that such a way of thinking was pretty old fashioned, but then, one could argue anything. For instance, one could make a case for the "now" generation along the lines of "tomorrow we may die." Or one could bet all on the future, as religionists did. But give her the past every time, because the past laid down the rules.

Oh sure, one could break the rules to a certain extent, but there were firm limits. Some things one simply couldn't do, like marry the lover killed in the war or invent the telephone—since Bell had already invented it. One couldn't change the past any more than one could call it back. The past heard no appeals.

She had a husband and a country upbringing, and that's how it was. She didn't cheat. She'd come close, though, by allowing Jon to kiss her. Once he saw how tempted she was, he had pressed the advantage. And he'd be back, if she knew her man.

Well, she wasn't going to risk another encounter. Indulgence was too easy a thing, and honor, too hard to come by. A person had obligations, especially a person like herself, lucky enough to overcome the adversity of a husband's permanent disability.

She loved Cal still, in his invalidism, although necessarily in a different way. And this difference opened the door to Jon, to romantic notions, to foolishness. Sure, he was good looking and bright and even charming in a shy-little-boy way. And there was something deeper, something mysterious and alluring about him. But so what? She just wouldn't go that route! Foolishness might be commonplace, but not for her!

Georgia, as a result of these reflections, packed her bags before going to bed and otherwise prepared for an organized departure. Thus when she awoke the next morning, her luggage stood neatly beside the door, while the sea-green ensemble she had selected for travel hung ready in the closet. It took almost no time at all to dress for the coming day.

She gave herself one final inspection in the mirror before going downstairs to breakfast. Her figure in the crocheted dress showed to its full, magnificent advantage. Men, at least, would overlook any trace of tiredness in her face for the spectacle of her body.

When she entered the dining room, Wally waved from a table by the window, then stood up. As she approached and sat down in the chair he held for her, his eyes covered her form in a manner reassuring as to men's priorities in assessing women's charms.

"You look great, Georgia." He signaled for the waiter, who brought coffee and took Georgia's order. "So you went out with Olsen."

"We had dinner with Peter and Deborah."

"I saw you going out the door, just you two," Wally informed her with a grin.

"That was afterwards. A walk to counter calories. What did you do last night?"

"Oh, had dinner and watched TV."

"Really?" she asked, sea-green eyes glowing. The coffee already had begun revitalization.

"They've got this singing gnome people throw confetti at. Uh, yeah, well, I took a walk, too." There was a pause while he spread butter on a Danish. "Did you get a chance to ask him what he's doing? Has he found what he came for?"

"He said he's working on an estate—which I reckon you know."

"What did he say about it?"

"Not much."

"Aw, come on!"

"Like I said, we were with Peter and Deborah. It wasn't a 'Mister-won't-you-tell-li'l-ole-me' situation."

Wally grinned again. "Not even afterwards?"

She glared at him. "'Afterwards' didn't take that turn either." Then she added flatly, "After breakfast, I'm going to get a flight out."

His eyes opened wide. "Jesus! What'd he do to you?"

"Don't be dumb, Wally."

He thought a moment and shook his head. "I can't believe you don't trip his trigger, so what gives?"

"I like him."

Wally whistled.

She asked, "And what will *you* be doing today?"

"Well, uh, seeing off Mr. Ratliff."

"Where's he going?"

Wally shrugged. "He buys the tickets."

"Why aren't you going with him?"

"He's coming back. Look, if you like Olsen, why don't you give it a whirl?"

"You'd like that, wouldn't you?" She smiled at him.

"Whaddaya mean?"

"Since you're after the same thing he's after, and you think I might distract him."

"You'd distract any man," he said gallantly.

"Odds are."

"Maybe I'd even cut you in."

"By yourself?"

He suddenly avoided her eyes. Obviously, it had been a slip. "A deal could probably be worked out," he muttered, spearing a choice bit of eggs Benedict with his fork.

"No, Wally. I don't want to hear about it."

"It's worth a nice bit of money," he challenged, meeting her gaze again.

"Honest. I'm taking the first flight I can get."

"He really got to you! Funny, I tabbed him as square and old fashioned on shipboard. He wore this old, goofy looking hat."

"Did he?" She smiled.

"Yeah. Very dated."

"Nothing's dated except fads and cereal boxes," she told him, as the waiter brought her order.

They ate in silence for a while, until he asked, "Have you told Mr. Ratliff? About leaving, I mean."

"I haven't seen him yet."

"But you will?"

"I certainly intend to say goodbye."

"There'd be no reason for you to mention, well, our conversation, I suppose."

"Reckon not," she replied.

He gave her a funny look. It seemed as if he might be going to unburden himself. He even took a deep breath, the way one does prior to confession. But he ended up toying with his coffee cup. They spoke instead of the Soviet submarines allegedly off Stockholm.

When finished eating, they walked to the lobby together, there to part. Wally strolled toward the main entrance and pushed through the doors to outside, an act in which he was soon followed by one of the three men seen often in Felix Ratliff's presence over the weekend. Georgia headed for the travel information desk to arrange a new flight. However, she was intercepted in this intention.

"Georgia, my dear," came Felix' voice from behind her. "How delightful you look."

"Thanks." She turned to him.

"Are you planning an outing?" and he indicated the travel desk.

"I'm about to change my tickets home, if I can."

"Oh, really? Going early? I hope nothing's wrong."

She smiled at him. "Just restless, I guess."

"Peter and Deborah going too?"

"Not that I know of."

"All alone?" There was a note in his voice quite divorced from courteous inquiry, and also from concern for her safety. It was a tone of doubt or skepticism or even exploitation.

She shrugged, a movement that necessarily called attention to her sexuality. "Looks like a solo flight, unless you want to come along."

"Ah! An irresistible invitation that I must nonetheless decline. But let me help you with your tickets," he offered, holding out his hand in anticipation, almost in demand.

She delved into her handbag, saying, "That's very nice. I'd like to go today. At least as far as I can get." She handed him the packet.

"As far as you can get?"

"Preferably all the way home."

"But as far as you can get, my dear?" he repeated, again with the note of cynical interest in his voice. "Does that include, say, Copenhagen?"

"Yes, Copenhagen."

"I fear something here displeases you very much. So sorry." His smile was ostensibly kind.

"No. No, if anything, the opposite."

"You're in flight from pleasure? Doesn't that strike you as odd, the way it strikes me?"

"I can't say it does, Felix."

"Rejection of pleasure's a Puritanical vice." He bent his eyes on her. "But I'll find you a passage all the way home, if the route doesn't matter."

She thanked him and started to accompany him the rest of the way to the desk, whereupon he assured her he could manage on his own.

"Perhaps you might like to settle your bill," he suggested.

She hesitated to follow his advice, since she did not share his confidence in the outcome of an affair at once so haphazard and so bureaucratic as changing airline tickets at the last minute.

She moved to the front of the lobby rather than to the cashier's domain. Looking outside, she noticed a well-dressed older man chatting with the doorman, who pointed toward the street in response to a question. The older man thanked him and walked down the front steps and crossed the street, looking to his right and to his left. Beyond him lay the park, the park where Jon had taken her in his arms so recently.... It was the same park where now she saw Wally Macleod strolling, to disappear into the mist thrown up by a large fountain at its center.

CHAPTER 18

▼

The well-dressed man Georgia had observed speaking to the hotel doorman entered the park from the east and approached the Carl Johan statue. The brim of his hat was pulled low, hiding his eyes, and, despite the increasing warmth of the day, he wore an ascot well up on his neck. The passing observer saw very little of his face and might, at best, remember his slightly stooped walk.

It was Rudi Anderson, in search of Wally, and he moved briskly in the direction indicated by the doorman. He found it disconcerting that the employee knew Wally Macleod and could point in the direction he had taken. Clearly the American had not kept a low profile at the hotel.

Rudi ignored a beautiful girl sauntering toward him and did not so much as glance at the fountain or the children playing in it. Breathing heavily from his exertion, he rounded the fountain and peered this way and that. Spotting a young man sauntering half a block ahead, he increased his pace as much as his years allowed. As he huffed along, he wondered, not for the first time, if he had made a wise choice agreeing to Wally as an ally. Sure, the young American could keep tabs on Felix Ratliff, but Rudi was not sure he possessed the mental discipline or the intelligence to carry out his part of the arrangement. And where would he find money for the eggs, if Ratliff were excluded? Of course, all such conjecture might well be pointless in light of this morning's horrifying discovery!

Deciding that the figure ahead was, indeed, Wally, Rudi followed after, still at a fast pace, still with labored breath. Slowly he gained on the younger man, who clearly was in no hurry as he paused to watch the play of the fountain, a spat between two children, and the sway of an attractive woman. In due course Rudi came within hailing distance, then closer, at which point Wally, alerted by the sound of his steps, wheeled and recognized him.

"What're you doing here!" he demanded, looking anxiously beyond the other's shoulder. "The hotel's full of people who shouldn't see us together!"

"A…minute," gasped Rudi, taking the time required for catching his breath.

"Who told you where to find me?" Wally demanded. "What if Felix saw you? Christ, we mustn't be seen together!"

"Something…terrible's happened!" exclaimed Rudi.

"Well, out with it!"

"My eggs!" he rasped, unable to say more.

"*Our* eggs!" Wally corrected. "What about them?"

"They're gone!"

"Gone!" Wally took him by the shoulders and shook him. "How can they be gone! How *can* they!"

"Gone!" cried Rudi despairingly. "Gone! Gone! Gone!"

CHAPTER 19

▼

It was almost twenty-four hours since Violet had discovered the apparition's portrait, the photograph marked "Jager Vaino 1920." She had not been entirely idle during that time. Besides dining with her cousins, she had discussed the discovery of the photo circumspectly with Anna after Jon's departure Sunday evening and had looked up certain topics in Yelena's German language encyclopedia.

"Look at this," she instructed, while thrusting the photo under Anna's nose. "What kind of uniform do you think that is?"

Anna, still working on Yelena's correspondence in the dressing room, set aside a letter to examine the picture. She did not omit looking at the caption on the back. "That's a Finnish name and a German title," she said. "The Germans trained Finnish soldiers to fight the Russians. He's probably one of them." She handed the portrait back.

"Oh, did they? The Germans, I mean. I'm not much for Finnish history."

"You ought to be. It's the only honorable history in the twentieth century. In Europe, anyway."

"Indeed!"

"Let me see that again," Anna said, looking once more at front and back. She returned the photograph without comment.

Although Violet found the silence of this action a little odd, she felt gratitude for Anna's information and almost immediately searched out the encyclopedia. From it she learned that a body of Finnish troops actually called the "Jagers" came from Germany to take part in Mannerheim's victory over the Reds. Then they seemed to disappear from history, or at least from the encyclopedia.

The article on Mannerheim himself did not mention the Finnish "Jagers," but rather was geared toward the subject's remarkable achievements. Quite justifiably, Violet decided. It seemed that at seventy-two he again took command of the Finnish army against the Reds—now Stalin's "Soviets"—and conducted a brilliant defense. At seventy-two she herself certainly didn't feel up to any winter campaign!

Nowhere in the encyclopedia did she find the name "Vaino"—not particularly surprising, but disappointing nonetheless. Nor was the word in the one gazetteer she could locate. According to her reference, the "Jagers" drew Finns from all classes, so possibly her apparition had been a commoner. If so, low birth did not prevent a regal pose.

She decided Vaino must have been a friend of Ingmar's, not Yelena's. They would have fought together under Mannerheim. Perhaps they still collaborated in 1925, when Vaino visited the Andersons in Christiana. Of course, if she read the encyclopedia rightly, under Mannerheim's intrepid leadership the Finns had finished the war by then. That fact didn't prevent the two men's remaining friends.

But why did the apparition—that is, Jager Vaino—hide? If he and Ingmar were friends, why did he appear at Yelena's when Ingmar was absent? Yes, there was something tricky about that. Either Vaino carried out a clandestine mission, or he was supposed to be somewhere else, or he pursued the exquisite Yelena. Or suppose Ingmar and he had temporarily exchanged identities, so that Yelena's husband might return to Russia for something important—for instance, Imperial Easter Eggs!

Violet liked the explanation about the Eggs, although it probably wasn't so. Why should it be so, especially when she'd been thinking so irrationally ever since arriving in Oslo? Useless recollections of Tryggvi were the main cause. Soured love made one crabby, and the more so when one turned every corner in Oslo with an insipid, girlish expectation of meeting the scoundrel!

Meet Tryggvi indeed! If not dead, he most assuredly inhabited an asylum. And even if, somehow, he had escaped detention, his bandy legs must have degenerated into arthritis and canes by now. Paunchy, probably, the sunlit hair turned to snow, with the inevitable, ill-fitting dentures!

Well, an old woman could be romantic, but the vessel of romance could never be an old man, and vice versa. The Tryggvi of today—even if he existed—must be treated as an object of pity or reverence, avoidance or inheritance, depending on how he'd turned out. Largely a matter of money, she supposed. She'd been silly to let memories of him take over.

What, after all, did memories represent? Merely one version of a past that occasionally hadn't even occurred. On the other hand, certain facts about the past lived on only in memory, and only so long as that particular memory persisted. It was all rather sad. She hated to think that with her own death, the romantic glamour of Tryggvi's manhood would totally cease to exist, just as if it had never been.

Nevertheless, since that was the case, one cherished memories, even at the peril of altering reality—as she'd been doing the past few days. Because Nature was such an incurable Romantic, one could blather around fairly indefinitely, until "saved" from delusion by cirrhosis or hailstones or whatever reality chose to break in on the fantasy. As Violet had been "saved" by the photograph of Vaino.

It recalled her to where she was, to what she was after. She wasn't thinking about Tryggvi any more, but about Finns and Russians, Faberge and Mannerheim, Rudi and Xenia. Yes indeed, about her Anderson cousins—the one so clearly disturbed by Felix Ratliff's coming to Oslo, and the other so very interested in Jon's activities. Why so, unless they wished the central pieces of Yelena's bequests for themselves?

And she was thinking about Jager Vaino, of course. What about him? Did his life add up only to this, a photograph? She rather thought not. Jon had said Vaino was the name of Yelena's friend on Bygdøy, and surely it was the same Vaino, the Jager Vaino.

Just at this point in Violet's reflections, as she sat behind Yelena's desk, there came the tell-tale click of the front door latch and then the almost eerie swinging inward of door on hinges. Xenia came into view, in the act of picking up a suitcase of rich-looking brocade. She crossed the threshold, suitcase in hand.

"Good mornink," she said, storing her suitcase just beyond the doorway leading to the back hall.

Violet remained seated. "You're earlier than usual," she remarked, not exactly accusingly.

"To make up for yesterday. I was so naughty, not comink back." Xenia glanced down at nothing in particular as she reached the desk. "So! How was Jon's evenink?"

"Oh, I haven't heard. I suspect we'll be lucky if he shows up at all today."

"What do you mean!" Xenia sounded alarmed.

"Just that he's not been very punctual so far."

"Ah! Let's call and see when he's comink. It's *his* plan, after all! He should be here to direct!"

"You think so?"

Xenia did not answer, for already she was dialing, to reach the hotel, but not Jon. After leaving a message, she said to Violet, "Maybe he is on his way."

"Maybe not." Violet had been studying Xenia, who displayed more agitation than usual. Not that Rudi's wife ever evidenced a deficiency in vitality. In that respect, she had always reminded Violet of silent film heroines who quick-marched through their scenes.

Xenia was saying, "Where would he be, if he's not in his room and he's not comink here?"

"With Mrs. Beech, I suppose."

"Mrs. Beech?"

"One of his paramours," stated Violet, from a residue of malice in her heart for Tryggvi's inconstancy.

Having no way of knowing that Mrs. Beech and the Georgia of last night's conversation were one and the same, Xenia exclaimed, "Paramours! But he has no right!"

At this, Violet eyed her curiously. She had the sudden suspicion Jon might have included Xenia, too, in his philandering. It was absolutely incredible, of course—so incredible nothing should ever surprise her again!

"No, no!" Xenia protested at once. "You mistake my meanink! Zere's nozzing like zat!"

"I'm glad to hear it."

"Certainly!" Xenia, sat down in a nearby chair and pulled it closer to Violet's. In a stage whisper, not without dramatic impact, she said, "I know where ze Eggs are hidden!"

Violet couldn't keep the shock from registering on her face.

"I know, and no one else!" Xenia declared.

"No one? Not Rudi?"

"No one else! Zey can never be found except zrough me! Or accident. And accident will take a very long time."

It struck Violet that Xenia was building up to something unpleasant, was about to display a serious defect in character, but she refrained from any comment.

"I see you're goink to be reasonable," Xenia said.

"Let's say, I'm listening."

"Jon should hear, too."

"Why do we need Jon?"

"It's to do with retrieving ze Eggs."

"Something about his height, I imagine," Violet surmised airily. In this challenging situation, she was thinking marvelously well, by far the best since arriving in Oslo. Tryggvi and all his distracting trappings had vanished, banished by the ever-so-much-more interesting novelty of Xenia's foray into extortion. "You should keep in mind the Eggs aren't Jon's. They're mine. Rudi's, too, I dare say."

Xenia shrugged. "Technically, zis might be right. But how can you own what you can't find?"

"And what about finding what you don't own?"

"Ze owners come off better if zere's a finder's fee," Xenia advised.

"Ah. And what would your finder's fee be, may I ask?"

Xenia drew a deep breath and held it briefly, while not removing her eyes from Violet's. Then she blinked, released the breath and answered, "One half ze Eggs."

"And if they're three? If they come in some inconvenient number?" Violet inquired without hesitation.

"An equitable adjustment."

"You don't require splitting an Egg down the middle?" Violet asked in a spirit of amusement, for she was aware of the irony of her ownership as much as to the presumption of Xenia's demand.

"Don't take me lightly!" exclaimed the younger woman, now looking both imperious and angry.

"Tut! If I take anything, it's offense. Why should Rudi have two thirds, and I, one, when we're equal heirs at law?"

"Rudi has nozzing to do wiz zis!"

"He's merely your husband."

"I have greater right zan eizzer of you!"

"I suppose you mean possession constitutes nine-tenths. Except you don't have possession. Unless I misunderstand, you require Jon's services to manage that." Violet eyed Xenia with more curiosity than hostility.

Now Xenia rose from her chair. She wore a bold, hard, commanding expression and flung out her hand, the forefinger pointing commandingly at the floor, as if she possessed the power to consign Violet to the hell below. "Enough!" she cried. "I'm Romanov! You and Rudi are nozzing!"

At first Violet drew a complete blank. She stared at the figure before her, at the curvaceous, erect generalissimo who had delivered such unexpected tidings. It flashed across her mind that Xenia must be mad. Then she remembered the family gossip about the time of Rudi and Xenia's marriage. Finally, acting as if this might be the perfect opportunity for inquiring into Xenia's genealogy, she asked, "Are you really? Which line?"

"Don't be supercilious!"

"Not at all. I'm very interested."

"Tatiana Nicholayevna."

"Tatiana?"

"Yes, my grandmozzer."

"And your grandfather?"

"Russian. A guard."

"A guard!" exclaimed Violet.

"A Red guard. He saved Tatiana from execution."

"Do you have proof?" asked Violet.

"Bah! How childish you are! What proofs did ze Revolution leave? Whole families, whole classes slain or deported! Orphans wizzout names! Papers and photographs stolen! No, I have no proofs! I have my mozzer's word!"

"Like the Dark Ages!" Violet murmured, momentarily swept up by Xenia's sense of drama. Shaking that off, she added, "But without proof..." and paused.

"I don't have to defend my descent! Who are you and Rudi? Not even Russians!"

Violet eyed Xenia, so fashionable, so hardy, so confident of self and heritage. It was just possible, of course, that she might be Romanov. Unfortunately, several million others could make the same claim with as much substance.

"Enough!" Xenia was saying. "I know where ze Eggs are. The location was in Yelena's papers—papers I've since lost, shall we say. So careless of me."

Violet refused to be distracted from making her own point. "Being a Romanov would make all the difference."

"We will discuss ze Eggs, please."

"If you're a Romanov, it wouldn't be through a Red guard. The Grand Duchess wouldn't marry such a person."

"You are crazy!" Xenia exclaimed.

"Of course she wouldn't! There used to be standards about such things."

"Ah!" A cynical expression crept into Xenia's face as she folded her arms and met Violet's gaze of feigned innocence.

They had reached an impasse of sorts. Violet only hoped Jon would appear soon to restore a semblance of reason.

CHAPTER 20

▼

Later that morning, following a long, sometimes rancorous talk with Xenia and Violet, Jon was able to persuade the women that their only hope lay in compromise and cooperation. Rudi was not entirely a fool, he averred—a judgment Xenia was loath to accept—and Felix Ratliff had Wally Macleod and possibly the KGB itself to draw from, so it behooved them to work rapidly and as a team if they hoped to get to the Eggs before the others did. It was possible that still others were hot on the trail, but when pressed for details and identities, Jon admitted to little more than suspicions.

In spite of his impassioned pleas, Jon saw mistrust burning in the eyes of both women, and almost an hour passed before Xenia revealed that they would have to go to Geneva to continue the search. In spite of their protestations, she would disclose nothing further, and so it was agreed they would return to their rooms and pack while Jon made reservations on the first flight out.

At the hotel Jon realized he had to work rapidly. There were only five hours until the plane took off for Geneva, and the order of business included collecting his belongings, paying the hotel bill, picking up the tickets, making things straight with Anna, picking up Aunt Violet, and above all, seeing Georgia Beech. Accordingly, once he reached his room, he walked directly to the telephone and dialed. However, the desk clerk at Georgia's hotel reported her out.

It took him almost no time to pack. Four hours and forty minutes remained when he went downstairs to pay for the room. Before making the short walk to the airline office, he tried Georgia's hotel again, but with the same result. When finally he returned to the room for his luggage, four hours and five minutes were left.

Once more he called Georgia's hotel, this time to be informed that Mrs. Beech had checked out. Checked out! Jon asked to be connected with Mr. or Mrs. Van Cleef, and in due course Peter came on the line.

He confirmed Georgia's departure and added, "She won't like it, but I'll tell you anyway. She's on a flight to Reykjavik at twelve fifty-seven."

"Why?" Jon asked in stunned bewilderment.

Peter came blessedly to the point. "You," he said.

"Damn!," Jon exclaimed, although thrilled in a way. After mumbling his thanks, he immediately began recalculating his agenda, with12:57 as a cutoff. An hour and a half had just been lopped off the schedule! He had less than two hours and twenty-five minutes to manage with Aunt Violet, Anna, and Georgia!

Calling the Embassy, he asked for Anna. The operator put him on hold. It seemed like forever, and he rearranged his billfold before a second voice suddenly addressed him over the telephone. Ms. Nygaard was in a meeting, the voice asserted. Then the connection was severed.

"Damn!" Yet he made the best of it by telling himself that canceling his meeting via an office operator's log would be incredibly bad form—unforgivable in fact. All the proprieties demanded that he talk to Anna herself. Nevertheless, he felt dismay upon looking at his watch: two hours and fifteen minutes to go!

Departing with luggage, he commandeered a cab, which promptly took him to Violet's hotel. His aunt was in her room, but far from ready. Without explaining much, he arranged to meet her at the Swissair counter at Fornebu around 1:30. He then left with two bags she wanted stored at Yelena's. He had tried to reach Anna again before going, but was unsuccessful.

Twenty more minutes had elapsed. He took another taxi and had the driver wait while he dropped Violet's extra baggage at Yelena's house, then wait again in front of the American Embassy. Jon entered the Embassy in a rush and was at once halted by a vigilant U.S. Marine, doubtless on suspicion of an imminent terrorist act.

"I just want to see Miss Nygaard. I've a message for her."

The Marine clearly measured Jon's contours for location of the bomb. "You'll have to wait here, sir."

"Look, I'm trying to catch a plane. Let me leave a message." He started reaching in his pocket, saw the Marine loosen the strap on his holster, and raised his hands instead, palms open, for the Marine to see. "I just need to write a message. I'm an American citizen. My passport's in the left, inside coat pocket."

From behind he heard Anna's voice. "Jon! Why do you have your hands up?"

"You know this gentleman, Ms. Nygaard?" the Marine inquired.

"Most certainly."

The Marine snapped to attention and departed, as Jon lowered his hands and Anna came closer, to peer up at him. "What's the story?" she asked.

"Look, I haven't time to explain." He glanced at his watch, seeing it was now nearing 11:30. "I'm flying to Geneva with Aunt Violet this afternoon. We're going to Lausanne, actually. I'll have to take a rain check for tonight. I'm sorry."

"I don't believe you. You're not sorry at all."

"Anna, I don't have time for...."

"*Why* are you going to Lausanne?" she asked, with her aseptic, clinical look.

"It's about Yelena's estate."

"And you're coming back?"

"Yes."

"When?" and she smiled in a way that reminded Jon of the silent violence of a Venus flytrap.

"As soon as we're done with our business." He tried unobtrusively to see his watch. Eleven thirty-two!

"What plane are you taking?"

He looked into her eyes again quickly. "Here." He produced his billfold and the envelope of tickets. "You can see for yourself, since you doubt me." Rather to his surprise, she took the tickets from their holder and examined them before giving them back.

"You don't leave for three hours," she said, and then added absently, "Faberge died in Lausanne. Did you know that?"

"No, I didn't know that."

"Maybe you ought to do a little more homework, Jon!" and she turned on her heel.

Even though pressed for time, he could not let her go on that note. Even though her manner offended him, he forgave for the sake of his own deficiency in handling awkward emotional situations like this one. Clamping his hands on her shoulders, he forced her around to face him. "I'm sorry!" he declared. "I'll be back. We can talk about all this then."

She looked at him defiantly a moment and, when he released her, fled. For a few seconds he stood rooted, following her with his eyes, then he glanced at his watch again. Eleven thirty-four!

Hastening from the Embassy, he entered the waiting cab. "To Fornebu," he directed. "As fast as you can make it!"

Sensing the spirit of adventure, of urgency, the cabby set out west along Drammensveien as if he were driving in the Grand Prix or in Mexico City. Such dispatch would have placed them at the airport an hour in advance of Georgia's flight, except that near a complicated intersection they found themselves in a traffic jam. It was advance, stop, advance, stop. And then just stop.

Although Jon approved the abstract principle of utilizing enforced leisure for constructive thought, he encountered difficulty applying the principle now. All he could do was keep looking at his watch. A desperate need to catch up with Georgia dominated him. He could not even consider such niceties as what to say or what to do, once they were reunited.

"Is there any way out of this?" he asked desperately, as they inched along again. Although the driver held out hope, Jon's watch continued to advance: eleven fifty-two, eleven fifty-three. Reaching a stretch of highway bounded by grass, the intrepid driver turned the wheel, plowed across a minor ditch and bumped over an incline to a lesser road. It was a demanding feat executed with skill, and they were once more on their way at three minutes after twelve.

Jon sat back and devoted the remaining minutes of the drive to contemplating detestable alternatives. Obviously Georgia was attracted to him, or she wouldn't be running away—the poles of the magnet, et cetera. As for him, he had never in his life wanted anything more urgently than bedding her. But where did fulfilling this inordinate desire lead, except to a shared loss of integrity, to moral illness?

The alternative—that is, *not* bedding her—seemed almost as unthinkable. How could he deny himself such pleasure simply because she already had a husband? Simply because a gentleman didn't force himself on a woman? Simply because no one lived happily ever after? Even allowing for his somewhat fevered state, restraint had to be judged a mental sickness....

He had reasoned only this far by twelve twenty-five, when they pulled up at the terminal. Tipping the driver outrageously—or perhaps not so outrageously, considering the cabby's performance—Jon hurried inside. He had half an hour to find her.

He began looking at the airline desk, then at the gate, then along the route from desk to parking lot, then back. All this he accomplished in slightly over ten minutes, while carrying his case. At twelve thirty-seven, returning toward the gate, he spotted ahead a certain unmistakable figure, just as the public address system broadcast a boarding call for the Reykjavik flight. He caught up with her at once. Seizing her arm, he impelled her to one side despite resistance.

"Hey! What're you doing? Let me go!"

"No." He had set down his suitcase and held her arms as in a vice.

"My plane!"

"Doesn't leave 'til twelve fifty-seven."

She gazed at him steadily from the luminescent sea-green eyes and stood very still.

"I love you, Mrs. Beech. Surely you know that."

"I reckon it'll pass. Like chicken pox."

Only then did he notice how tensely she held herself, how the wise-cracking words must belie her true feelings. "Is this it?" he asked perceptively. "Is this the lie you said I wouldn't recognize?"

She remained stiff, unyielding. "Think what you will."

At last he sighed in resignation. "Okay, we'll do it your way. But there's such a thing as good manners."

"I'm kinda counting on that, to tell the truth."

"Upholding civilization, all that sort of thing," he amplified, while relaxing his grip and taking her in his arms. "All that sort of thing," he repeated, letting his eyes rove over her face.

Elusively, she laid her cheek against his chest.

"It's no use, Georgia. I know you're leaving because you don't want to deal with this thing between us." He looked at the cascading curls within his arms, against his chest, and saw no motion. "We can't say goodbye without a proper goodbye kiss," he urged. But still she did not move.

He gave her another moment, then warned, "Tell you what. If you don't kiss me goodbye, if you don't observe the proprieties, I'm going to fly to Stomping Ground, Kentucky, and drown your husband in the nearest lake!"

At that, she raised her head, promptly to be given his "proper good-bye kiss"—actually quite a showy concoction that captured the attention of all bystanders as well as the parties involved. Afterwards he said, "I don't know…" not letting her go.

"I've got to catch my plane," she reminded, in a kind of whisper.

"I just don't know. I imagine I'll come to Stomping Ground after all."

She shook her head. "Goodbye, Jon."

"Well, I may." He released her gradually.

She smiled. "So long. Best of luck." She turned on her heel, but he glimpsed the tears shimmering in her eyes. He knew this was costing her as much as it was him.

Nevertheless, at that moment, he felt almost mortally deprived. He was sorely tempted to haul her back, and to hell with airline schedules, with Geneva and Reykjavik, with husbands and aunts! Such were his impulses, but he did not act upon them because he suddenly realized he was being watched.

As Georgia left his arms, he saw a man across the way observing them—an unobtrusive sort of man, with a bland, forgettable face, who joined the intervening crowd of travelers after Jon's eyes met his. Jon caught sight of him again, once Georgia disappeared from view. He followed in the direction taken by the stranger, but the man had vanished. His eyes swept the concourse, but without result. As it was now past one o'clock, he elected to discontinue this search in favor of getting himself in order for the adventure to come.

At the appointed time for meeting, Violet appeared at the Swissair counter where Jon waited. Her first words were, "*Will* you explain what all this rummaging is about!"

"I was seeing someone off. Did you have any trouble getting here?"

"Did you get my luggage to Yelena's?" she countered.

"Yes, ma'am."

"Well, *whom?*"

"I beg your pardon?"

"*Whom* were you seeing off?"

"Mrs. Beech."

"Oh!" She peered at him suspiciously. "Are we meeting her in Lausanne?"

"No."

She looked both sympathetic and relieved, then asked, "Do you think we've made the right decision, going along with Xenia? Such a scheming minx!"

"I doubt we'll find the Eggs without her."

"So it seems. Oh, but imagine seeing them again, seeing things buried from sight for forty years! That's marvelously exciting!" Her eyes snapped with enthusiasm at the prospect.

By contrast, Jon's narrowed suddenly, and he muttered something under his breath.

"What did you say?"

"Nothing," he insisted, while checking the baggage through. This caused Violet to look at him repeatedly and impatiently like a child at a man known to have a pocketful of candy.

As soon as they left the counter, she demanded, "Tell me!"

"Over there," he replied, guiding her to an out-of-the-way corner without potential eavesdroppers. The man caught spying remained very much on Jon's mind at this point.

"So?" she asked, when they had reached the corner.

"Anna told me something very interesting a few hours ago."

"You've seen her, too? Jon, you're old enough you really should pace yourself!"

"You may be right," he temporized, to forestall her lecture. "Anyway, Anna said Faberge died in Lausanne."

Violet's expression shifted kaleidoscopically from mere interest to revelation to high excitement. She exclaimed, "How perfectly splendid! Marshal Mannerheim died there, too! I've just been reading about him! The Finnish leader, you know. Isn't that odd! What does it mean?"

Jon shrugged, because he felt a little disappointed, or at any rate, miffed. The way his thoughts had been tending, two deaths held less significance than one. Aloud he said, "Perhaps it's just coincidence. When did Mannerheim die?"

"Oh, after the war. The Second World War. And of course Faberge died shortly after World War One. But it means something! I know it in my bones! Just like I have this dreadful intuition Xenia's up to something illegal!"

"Such as?"

"I don't know. It's already extortion, you see. And then there's Rudi, the matter of cutting him out. I don't know exactly how the law terms her conduct *there*, but it must be some kind of breach. Breach of trust? Or maybe it's embezzlement!" Her expression was almost gleeful.

He thought she might be getting too manic, that she needed something to sober her up. He said, "I think you should realize we're dealing with a thief."

"You're calling Xenia a thief? When she says she's a Romanov?"

"Caligula said he was a god, and you know how that panned out."

"Oh dear!"

"Aunt Violet, regardless of how distasteful it is, you must recognize that, once she's led us to the Eggs, she must be discarded."

Violet's eyes became huge. "You mean eliminated?"

He smiled. "You've read too many detective stories."

"But 'discarded?' It's like breaking our word." She fiddled with her lapel, then murmured, "You're too hard. Like Hia. Like your mother."

"You can leave it safely to me, then."

"But it comes to the same thing."

"Yes," he agreed, "the same thing."

She frowned and picked at the strap of her handbag. Then she sighed. Finally she said, still playing with the strap, "All right. Do her in. You have my permission."

"It's not *that* bad."

"Yes it is. All her dreams will be broken."

"Well, dreams often end up that way...."

She raised her eyes to his. Hers were snapping so, they seemed to send out sparks. "You haven't an ounce of romance in you!" she declared, "Not an ounce!"

"Is that what you think?" he answered. His voice was soft.

CHAPTER 21

▼

As is the custom with most airlines, the lower orders were allowed on board the Swissair flight to Geneva only after first class had been seated—an arrangement that struck Jon as illogical inasmuch as the tourist-class passengers would subsequently plow through first class on the way to the rear, bags banging into seats that appeared twice as wide and three times as plush as those reserved for them. The only consolation in this absurd arrangement was that upon arrival, passengers departed in the same order they had entered, thus allowing first class to exit without again being buffeted by their inferiors.

In any event, Violet, Xenia, and Jon progressed down the isle slowly, stacked up behind passengers shoving carry-on luggage into overhead compartments and arranging children in their seats. It was a halting progression that gave Jon, with his penchant for observation, ample time to note the first class passengers on each side of the isle. Although he could not see their faces—most were buried in books or magazines, or were staring out the small windows—he could at least observe their mode of dress and, occasionally, their hats.

He was most struck by a slender, elegant young man seated by a window in front of the bulkhead. This person, whose hands were perfectly manicured, sported a black, wide-brimmed, flat-crowned hat with a red plume jutting from it, rather like a caballero of Spain or

Argentina. The hat was complemented by an elegant dark jacket, dark slacks, and black leather boots. Jon could not see the youth's face because of the wide hat, but he could see the end of a small but elegant black mustache curling slightly at the tip. He deduced that the youth was an artist or actor, one who perhaps wanted to remain anonymous while traveling but was unable to hide a basically flamboyant nature.

In the tourist section, a certain tension existed between Xenia on the one hand and Violet and Jon on the other. Neither party would allow the other out of sight. Thus all three sat in the rear, near the galley, where three consecutive seats remained available. Visits to the washroom were regarded with something akin to suspicion by all three, and were carefully watched.

An uneventful flight was followed by the chaos of luggage retrieval in Geneva and a long walk to the terminal carport where they hoped their rental car awaited. Just as they reached the entrance, Jon noted the elegant youth climbing into the driver's seat of a sporty red Audi and roaring off on the road to Lausanne.

When their BMW was brought around, Xenia insisted on sitting in the back, together with her tapestry suitcase. Jon put the other luggage in the trunk and then wedged his frame into the driver's seat. One of the many penalties for being six-foot-five is the discomfort of most European car designs. Thus they set out with Xenia in the back, Violet in the front passenger seat, and Jon adjusting his driving position all the way to Lausanne.

A problem immediately surfaced with regard to the rearview mirror. No seat adjustment would provide Jon a practical view of the goings-on behind him, forcing him to rely on the side mirrors to ascertain when someone wanted to pass on the winding, mountainous road. This loss to safe driving was Jon's gain, since it allowed him to concentrate on the spectacular Swiss scenery. Violet and Xenia exclaimed on the beauties of nature all the way to Lausanne, never once speaking of upcoming business.

Not far from Lausanne, they overtook the red Audi, parked at the side of the road, the elegant youth peering through binoculars at distant snow-capped peaks. As Jon managed a sharp curve he glanced at his side mirror and thought he saw the youth's binoculars trained on their car, but decided he was simply studying the inspiring view of Lausanne ahead. Indeed, it was a sight of awesome beauty, its collection of red-roofed houses nestled between the mountains and white-capped Lake Geneva.

Entering Lausanne, Xenia gave directions with frequent reference to a city map. At last they located the Pension Hubert, where Violet had booked three rooms. They had to wait several minutes for a space to clear in front of the pension, thus blocking a lane on the narrow street. A gray Russian Zis, which Jon had seen behind them on the road from Geneva, honked and passed on the right. Both Jon and Violet looked that way, to see three inscrutable Slavic faces staring back at them before disappearing down the picturesque street that oozed Old World charm.

They were a while getting settled at the Pension Hubert, but eventually set out on foot for a nearby restaurant Xenia recalled from a previous visit. The restaurant offered German fare: red cabbage, sauerbraten, celery root. Violet pronounced the food tolerable, provided one liked that sort of thing. Xenia proposed they go elsewhere for a walk and after-dinner drink, since nothing could be done with regard to their mission until the morrow.

Violet voiced the opinion that Jon might like that, after a day folded up in airplane and car seats. "As for me, I'd rather read." She spoke a bit snippily, as she sometimes did when age interfered with indulging her true preferences.

Xenia made no objection to leaving Violet alone at the pension, even though surveillance of her must thereby necessarily cease. So while Xenia and Jon began walking, Violet inquired at the front desk about open libraries or public lectures within a few blocks of the pension. Overhearing her question, a young man standing nearby informed her that a famous Swiss professor was lecturing on "German-Russian cultural bridges" less than two blocks away. Violet looked him up and down, raised her eyebrows questioningly, and thanked him for the information. The bystander had chosen odd attire for evening: he wore gold and green striped knickers.

Meanwhile Xenia and Jon proceeded along steep, narrow streets, none the less picturesque for electric lighting, which lent the scene a certain ambiguity. One half expected men sporting doublets and drawn swords to appear; alternately, blue jeans and switchblade knives. Either seemed possible in a setting distinctly of two times.

The busy bar they found enjoyed a clientele strictly from the twentieth century, many of them displaying straightened teeth, professional haircuts, artificial tans, and gold chains. They received a table for two next to a wall, and almost at once Xenia began evaluating the nationalistic implications of ordering wine versus beer. As she chatted, Jon let his eyes wander over the crowd at intervals.

"I don't zink you're listenink," she said at one point, and he offered a mild defense, to which she replied, "You're a gentleman and a scoundrel."

"The expression's 'gentleman and scholar'."

"You're a scoundrel."

He considered that a moment, before asking, "Why do you say that?"

"You reject my right."

"Your right?"

"To ze Eggs," she explained simply. Then more complexly, "I can't trust you."

"Maybe not. I'm interested only in preserving Aunt Violet's share."

"Ah! Ze last honorable man!" she laughed.

"*Somebody* has to have honor."

She laughed again, and then suddenly excused herself, to go to the restroom, she said. Standing, Jon watched her rise and head toward the back of the restaurant, until a man against the opposite wall distracted his eye. It was the stranger who had been observing him in the Fornebu terminal. Before he could decide what to do, he saw another man rise from a nearby table and follow Xenia from the room. For a moment he thought the man was Rudi, for he walked slightly bent at the waist, like a watchmaker who had spent too much time at his bench. But that was clearly impossible, inasmuch as Xenia's husband was still in Oslo. By the time he turned his attention back to find the first man, he had disappeared.

Jon took his seat, and after ten minutes or so, Xenia returned, looking flushed—or newly rouged. He did not mention the Fornebu stranger he had seen in the restaurant, and she seemed preoccupied and flustered. Very shortly thereafter, she suggested they leave.

Back at the pension, he saw Xenia to the door of her room. "'Til nine tomorrow," she said.

He waited until he heard her slip the bolt, then moved down the hall to his aunt's room. Lifting his hand to knock, he at the last moment thought better of it. Considering the hour and the day's activity, Aunt Violet was probably asleep.

CHAPTER 22

▼

Jon, Violet, and Xenia had taken few pains to keep secret their flight to Geneva. Indeed, Jon's scene with Georgia Beech at Fornebu terminal had drawn so much public scrutiny that any hope of secrecy must necessarily have been abandoned. Thus it was not surprising that Wally Macleod, who had been informed of their plans by agents of Felix Ratliff, had made his way to Geneva and thence to Lausanne at practically the same time the others arrived. What the Soviet agents did not know, Wally was convinced, was that he brought Rudi Anderson with him. And to insure that their little secret remained hidden, they traveled separately on the plane as well as in vehicles to Lausanne.

Rudi and Wally had previously agreed that if Jon, Violet, and Xenia split up, Wally would follow Violet Strasser. This arrangement reduced the chances of being detected, since Violet had never laid eyes on him. Thus when Violet was left at the pension by Xenia and Jon, it was Wally who scurried into the lobby to commence his conversation with her about "German-Russian cultural bridges," while Rudi shadowed Jon and Xenia.

With a young American's misconception of how to blend into the locale, Wally had elected to wear knickerbockers—or as his salesman had referred to them, plus fours—upon reaching Lausanne. Of course, the selection made him stand out, and particularly so at night. When he had told Violet about the fabricated "cultural bridge" lecture, she had looked him up and down with what seemed a degree of skepticism. Nevertheless, because of her desire to learn more about the deaths of Faberge and Mannerheim in Lausanne, Wally was able to keep her interested in the discussion.

Before coming to Geneva, Wally had discussed with Rudi the pro's and con's of kidnapping Violet, should the opportunity present itself. Although Rudi had at first objected to such action, he soon came round to Wally's view. They perceived her as the easiest prey among the three prospects to manage and also as the most likely to provide leverage in dealing with the other two. Jon, especially, might be expected to react protectively where his aunt was concerned and abandon his search for the Eggs.

Now Wally decided to act on his plan, for he volunteered to escort Violet to the lecture he had invented. Perhaps demonstrating a belated prudence about accompanying a stranger, she asked him further questions. Would they be talking about "heavy" history, or delightful snippets? Was it to be a nationalistic, self-congratulatory sort of lecture, or a local, gossipy one? And did he, by the way, happen to know where Faberge lay buried?

To the first two questions Wally responded in the way he hoped her wishes tended. The third he answered by saying, "No. But I'll find out."

"Oh, would you?" She seemed delighted by his interest.

"Of course." He paused, trying to appear thoughtful. "Come to think of it, the lecturer will probably be able to tell us."

At that point, Wally knew he had her hooked. And without showing much good sense, she set out with him from the pension.

He led her down several side streets until they reached what appeared to be an industrial area where all activity had ceased for the evening. He had brought a roll of tape to bind her wrists and cover her mouth. Fishing it from his pocket, he searched for a spot to conceal her until he could return later with an automobile. Perhaps that is why he did not see or hear the youth in the flamboyant hat dash past Violet, grab him by the arm, and jerk him around. He had only a moment to notice the theatrically curling black mustache before the youth struck him with the butt of a Magnum revolver. Wally dropped to the ground like a loosely packed sack of rice.

*   *   *   *

When Xenia excused herself to leave Jon in the bar, she expected Rudi to follow, for she had spotted him at his table some minutes earlier, trying to appear inconspicuous. He did not disappoint her. She waited under a dimly burning wall lamp in the passageway to the restrooms. Upon seeing him, she motioned with her head and began moving down the passage until she came to the exit and let herself out. Rudi followed, to find himself on the street.

She went on the offensive at once, as if he were the guilty party, as if she were the aggrieved. "What are you doing here?"

"What've you done with the eggs?" he countered, with a flexing motion of his hand.

"They're mine!" she hissed. "You've no right to them!"

"Yours!" He looked as if he might cry or scream or strangle her. "I *created* them! Are you mad?"

"Ze *real* Eggs are mine. Your baubles are nozzing without me."

"Don't waste my time with your rantings. I spent years designing and crafting those eggs, and I won't allow you to take them."

"I already have," she pointed out. This statement of unassailable fact seemed to dampen his rage somewhat, and Xenia continued, "Zey are not so bad. But can zey pass for real Faberge? Can zey fool Felix Ratliff?"

He appeared stunned. "How do you know about Ratliff?"

"Any fool can connect ze dots, Rudi. You are not so clever as you zink."

He glared at her but said nothing, apparently deep in thought.

Xenia repeated, "Can zey fool Ratliff?"

"Perhaps, under the right circumstances. After all, he is a buyer, not an artisan." After a pause he added, almost reluctantly, "I have a plan."

"I also have one." She looked at him expectantly.

"It's possible they are the same plan." Rudi was now miraculously calm, seeming to favor an attitude of cooperation. "'Wolves of the same pack....'"

"What does zat mean?"

"An old Finnish saying. Never mind. What is your plan?"

"Your eggs must be combined with ze real ones"

"Ah! And how might we arrange that?"

"I can arrange it. I know where zey are."

"Ah!" this time in a higher pitch.

Xenia hastened to explain that she planned to mingle Rudi's eggs with the Imperial ones, which were here in Lausanne, in a place only she knew. She added, not insincerely, "Perhaps you can be of help."

"I'm not alone."

"What do you mean, 'not alone?' Who's with you!"

"The American, Wally Macleod."

She threw up her hands. "What insanity!" she spat.

He drew himself up, became very straight. "It's not insanity. It's necessity. My eggs were gone. I had to tell him something."

"So you said I was a thief!"

"What else? Besides, Wally has his uses. He's probably kidnapping Cousin Violet right now."

"You are mad!" cried Xenia.

"No!" he corrected, "It means control over Jon."

"Ah!" She eyed him reflectively. "You may be right."

And he echoed, possibly in a spirit of mockery, "Ah!"

In a moment she said, "But we must work togezzer."

"That goes without saying."

"Tell zis Macleod nozzing. Put him off somehow—get rid of him—and come alone to the pension tomorrow night. By sundown."

"Then what?"

"You can follow us to ze hiding place."

"You said you know where the Eggs are," reminded Rudi.

"I do."

"And you're taking our cousins with you? Is this wise?"

"It is necessary. We've made a deal. I get half. Cousin Violet splits ze other half with you. Of course, she wants to be there, to see them."

Rudi folded his arms across his chest. "One half for you?" Then disapprovingly, "I see."

Xenia guessed he did not see at all. "Three fourths for *us*!" she revised. "And a lovely flat in Paris."

"Hm. And Cousin Jon?"

"He is not to be trusted. That's where you step in, if it becomes necessary. Agreed?"

He did not answer at once. Most likely he was working over her plan in his mind, quite possibly in hopes of discovering variations more favorable to himself. It was no less than she expected.

Perhaps he found one, for when he finally answered, it was resolutely: "Let's do it!"

"Good! Until tomorrow night zen," she said, retrieving her purse and leaving him in the alley.

*   *   *   *

The inconspicuous man, whom Jon nonetheless had spotted at the Oslo terminal and later in this very bar, tossed some francs on the table and followed Xenia and Jon out. He walked over to a parked Fiat, while keeping his eye on the cousins as they proceeded at a leisurely pace down the street. The Fiat's occupant rolled down the window and inquired in Russian, "Well?"

"They're probably calling it a night," answered the other, letting himself in the back seat. "But let's make sure."

They drove well behind the strollers, stopping when necessary, not using the lights. It was, as the inconspicuous man pointed out, "an easy tail." They chatted idly: about the passenger's flight from Oslo, about the driver's opinion of Geneva as a foreign post, about Felix Ratliff as an employer. Then the passenger remarked that Rudi Anderson had disappeared from the restaurant, probably after meeting his wife somewhere.

"How do you figure?" asked the driver.

"She left, he followed, then she returned."

"In it together, are they?" asked the driver.

"Looks that way. Mr. Ratliff will be interested in hearing all this."

"Yeah."

At no time did the anonymous man mention the mustachioed youth in the flamboyant hat, despite seeing him on the plane and once in Lausanne. After all, Lake Geneva was notorious for its artistic, film, and gay communities, and this seemed but another member of one of them.

*   *   *   *

The next morning Jon tapped at Violet's door and received no response. Assuming she had already gone to breakfast, he descended the stairs at a fast clip and entered the modest dining room. A quick survey established his aunt's absence. He felt the merest twinge of irritation as he sat down and ordered breakfast for one.

Because Violet never appeared, Jon returned upstairs after breakfast and again knocked on her door. Just as before, there was no answer. He then retraced his path downstairs, to stop at the small desk between staircase and dining room. However, the attendant had no knowledge of Miss Strasser's plans, nor any messages for Jon.

Thoroughly annoyed now, he went outside for a short walk that extended into a longer one. He was feeling put out, and not entirely in reaction to his aunt's apparent independence. Georgia was on his mind. The thought of her had kept him awake much of the night. As a matter of fact, not even a half-hour of push-ups and sit-ups at three in the morning had banished her. And as for his dreams....

Wandering into an area of modern shops, he looked in the windows for some time. When he came to a bookstore, he entered and soon located the history section. Because famous men's names tend to be the same in almost any language, he began browsing for something on Faberge.

Luck proved with him. He happened upon an English-language biography of sorts. Apparently intended for the coffee-table trade, it featured many color plates. His search for information ended with the revelation that Faberge's remains were removed from Lausanne to Cannes in 1930. This came as a disappointing surprise to Jon, who had settled on the theory that the Imperial Easter Eggs might be found in Faberge's grave.

He returned to the pension in a black mood, although he took his usual care not to show emotion. As he crossed the threshold, the desk clerk called, "*M'sieur! M'sieur* Olsen!" and proceeded to advise that Madame Xenia Anderson desired his presence immediately. She waited in her room for him.

"And where's Miss Strasser?" he asked the clerk.

"I'm sure I don't know, *m'sieur*."

"No messages?"

"No, m'sieur."

"Then I think we should let ourselves in, if she doesn't answer my knock. My aunt's no longer young."

The somber implications of this remark caused an almost comical raising of the clerk's eyebrows. "*Mon Dieu!*" he murmured, in a tone that suggested one couldn't have such things at the Pension Hubert.

Nevertheless, he trailed Jon upstairs. When Jon's knock once again elicited no response from Violet, the two men exchanged glances. Then Jon nodded almost imperceptibly, and the attendant inserted one of his keys in the lock.

Leading the way in, the clerk announced with a relief that sounded like triumph, "You see! She is out, *M'sieur!*" for there was no corpse on floor or bed.

Jon did not reply at first. He was taking note of the turned down bed that had not been slept in and Violet's walking shoes beside the nightstand, which indicated she was not out for a morning stroll. Only after this review did he say, with outward calm, "We'll have to check with the maid, of course, but it looks as if she's been out all night. As if she never returned from her activities."

*　　*　　*　　*

An hour after Jon established the fact of Violet's disappearance, Wally Macleod awoke with a groan in a hospital bed. Because he had sustained a near-concussion as well as the loss of his billfold, the authorities had no way to identify him. Thus the nurses greeted his return to the conscious world with noisy chatter. "English?" they kept asking, presumably because of the ridiculous trousers removed at his arrival.

In due course he got across his nationality, not to say his name and sundry other pertinent points. The plain clothes Swiss police officer assigned to investigate the assault concluded that a street robber had victimized Mr. Macleod. "Probably on dope, *M'sieur*, probably a Turk," the officer theorized, and immediately went on to speak of the complications caused by Wally's missing passport. Regrettably, Mr. Macleod would have to come to the police station after his release from the hospital, to straighten things out.

As soon as the officer left, Wally tried to call Rudi at their hotel. Rudi was not there, and he had to be content with leaving a message as to his own whereabouts. Clearly, he was going nowhere for a while.

CHAPTER 23

▼

The villa above Lausanne had that clean, bright look of the upper altitudes, as if snow still washed its windows even in summer, even under bluish skies and white sun. It lay flat and long upon its lesser prominence, where once a forest grew. House and pool and driveway and lawn all seemed imbedded in the side of the mountain, so lending themselves an air of permanence.

Once a small mental hospital for the privileged, then a civil defense installation for the Swiss military, the villa still bore evidence of its former lives in the bars on the west wing's windows and in the revolving turret over the center hall. In the 1960's, Jäger Vaino had purchased it and replaced the sturdy, protective south walls of the public rooms with large picture windows that afforded an excellent view of Lake Leman.

The villa belonged entirely to Vaino now—that same Vaino whose nameplate marked the house on Huk terrasse in Oslo, whose photograph Violet had identified in Yelena's house. Once he had shared the villa's ownership with Ingmar Anderson, and subsequently with Ingmar's wife, until she died. Yes, now even Yelena was dead.

Only Vaino remained among those who took part in the great adventure, in the final catastrophe surrounding the Tsar's death. Until very recently, he had believed that with his own death, the entire stirring episode would disappear from existence, from the collective memory called history. He had believed that as each participant departed this world, each took the secret with him. Yelena, too.

She had not wished to be buried in the meadow with husband Ingmar. Or rather, she had not wanted her grave in that place that bore such painful reminders of the tragedy. A matter of delicacy, she said, so that Vaino himself finally questioned whether to lie there, in the third space reserved for him. It was perhaps not right; he ought to consider a grave with Yelena in Oslo. It would be unseemly to leave her in the urn upstairs, unattended after his death.

Waiting to die, Vaino swam every day. At eighty-six, he could do it. He had always had a hardy constitution. He had endured the snows of Finland and Russia, under the stress of injury and battle, through the heartbreak of loss and extinction. It seemed inevitable that he should be the last, that he should outlive even the magnificent Yelena.

The swimming kept him relatively fit, and so prolonged his life. Besides, ever since that odd girl approached him at Yelena's cremation, he had something new to think about. He found amusement in telling her everything, of revealing the long, sad tale. But most interesting of all was the realization that he might not have needed to tell, that she had already figured out the essentials for herself. Such a beautiful girl. American, and disarmingly smart. Perhaps, if he did not die this season, he would return to Oslo and look her up.

CHAPTER 24

▼

Of course, long before Xenia hauled him about Lausanne in search of shovels and ropes, Jon had deduced they were after buried treasure somewhere in the vicinity. It had to do with Xenia's insisting he be a member of "the team" and with Anna's saying Faberge died in Lausanne. Jon was smart enough to sense when the services demanded of him might be a laborer's brawn rather than an engineer's brain. Similarly, he had more than enough logic and imagination to connect Faberge Eggs with Faberge's grave. But his visit to the bookshop that morning killed the idea—beautiful in its simplicity—of finding Faberge's grave and beating Xenia to the "lost" Eggs.

Almost immediately thereafter, he was confronted with Violet's disappearance. To the discomfort of the Pension Huber clerk, Jon reported her absence to the police, who checked the local hospital without result. While this finding did not automatically rule out stroke or some other sudden, natural debility, it tended to encourage theories of foul play. Thus he did not like at all Xenia's response to his news about Violet.

"Really! Do you zink somebody makes her hostage to keep you in line, darlink?" It sounded remarkably like a threat.

Outwardly Jon showed no emotion, but inwardly he seethed. The act of relinquishing Georgia had dangerously strained his composure.

Foul play involving his aunt might crack it! He felt enormous hostility toward Xenia, whom he now suspected of complicity in Violet's disappearance. He was on the verge of throwing constraint to the wind and pounding somebody.

He believed in the gentleman's code, in playing by the rules, but there were times when he wearied of his lifelong gentleness, when he resented the obligations of the strong to the weak. At such times it was not a case of right and wrong; it was a matter of power and will. All his tremendous self-control could not erase from his mind the awareness of his considerable strength—that he required no more than his hands to maim or kill.

Thus he bided his time, as they shopped for digging tools during an afternoon that passed with no word of Violet. At dinner, Xenia hinted further at a link between the missing Violet and Jon's obedience. He maintained his ostensible cool on the outside and fumed on the inside.

After dinner, because the summer days still were long, he had plenty of light to pack the car. Rope, shovels, torches, hammer, saw, crowbar, tape, lumber—all found a niche in the rented BMW.

"You're not an engineer for nozzing," Xenia told him approvingly.

In addition to her handbag and wrap, she kept a large canvas sack and the torches inside the car with her. The torches, smelling powerfully of resin, formed a physical barrier between Jon in front and Xenia behind—not unlike the mental reservations separating them.

"So where are we going?" he asked from the driver's seat. By now the sun was setting.

Caged away by the long torches, Xenia had put the sack on the floor by her feet. She was busy arranging her wrap. "Turn on ze engine and I will direct you."

"Where're we going?"

"I don't trust you."

"No?" and he looked down at her over the obstructing torches, his face impassive, the blue gray eyes steady.

She laughed, perhaps a little uneasily. Clearly she felt uncomfortable sharing so small a space with so large a man under adversarial circumstances. "No," she finally said. "I have ze itinerary here," pointing to her forehead.

Soon they were moving through Lausanne's streets, with Xenia as guide. Rather quickly they left the city behind, its lights fading in the rearview mirror. The foothills blocked out the dying sun, so that where mountains had loomed, a blackness hung. It became a case of sensing the Alps' presence from the grade and crookedness of the road.

The tension between them increased. Jon heightened it when he said, "Suppose someone's discovered the hiding place before us. Suppose the Eggs are gone."

"Nonsense! Only I know where zey are!"

"That's an assumption we must hope is true." In a moment he told her conversationally, "We're being followed. Somebody's been tailing us for quite some time."

"What!" and she turned to look out the rear window. "I don't see anyone!"

"He's just now veering off the road, to the right."

"Zen it's nozzing!"

"Oh, it's more than nothing," he disagreed. "Whoever it was followed us out of Lausanne."

"I can't see what's happened," she reported over her shoulder. "Maybe he went over ze side!"

"Maybe."

Xenia kept peering back, as though anticipating something.

"Was it Rudi?" Jon asked. Then more cruelly, "Was it good old Rudi who 'went over ze side'?"

She whirled around and glared at him. "Rudi!" she spat. "Why would you zink so?"

Not responding, he kept his eyes on the road. The sack at her feet crackled dryly as she reached for something inside. Then he felt the prod of steel against his neck.

He took his time about responding. "I'd raise my hands," he said, "but they're needed on the wheel."

"Bastard!" She pressed the gun harder against his neck. "Was it Rudi?"

"I don't know."

"Why did you say so?"

"Just exploring the probabilities."

"Bastard!"

They remained silent until Xenia suddenly directed him off the highway, onto a secondary road. At that point he told her he didn't like the gun pressed against his neck. "If it goes off, we may both end up in the ravine."

Withdrawing her weapon beyond the torches, she advised, "Just remember I'm still holdink it!"

He was not likely to forget, although he felt safe for the time being from anything but an accidental discharge of the weapon. She needed his services more than he needed hers. Once she had led him to the place, the advantage would change, at least temporarily.

She warned him to go slower, to watch for a wayside shrine.

"That's the place?"

"Sorry, darlink. Only a place on ze way," she answered mockingly, as if she knew what he was thinking.

It was not long before she cautioned him again to slow down, and also to be prepared to turn right. Almost at once they came upon a crossing. On one corner a stand of trees backed up to a solo shrine—boxy, like an upright coffin.

"Here!" she commanded. "Turn!"

This put them on a dirt road, rutted and very bumpy, so that their gear and the car itself rattled and clattered, to drown out any other sounds the night may have offered.

They came to a divide in the road. Xenia directed him to the left. Within a minute the trail petered out, and their headlights revealed what appeared to be a meadow, bordered by firs. As he brought the car to a halt, Xenia scrambled out, pointing the gun at him. "Yes! Zis is it!"

By now the moon had risen, to dispel the earlier cloak of morbid darkness. Jon killed the lights, and after a few moments he could make out the scene more completely than before: a small meadow, edged by tall firs, and toward the right, three gravestones, one taller than the others. Xenia walked rapidly to them and stood by the tall one. She was stroking it. As he left the car and began his approach, she wheeled and leveled the gun menacingly at him. A moonbeam struck the barrel, and he stopped.

"Bring ze torches!" she ordered.

He brought the torches, thrusting them firmly in the ground where she directed, and set them afire. As they snapped to life and cast their flickering light across the largest of the stones, he read aloud the name chiseled there: "Anderson."

"Ingmar's grave," she told him, "And someone else."

"Cousin Ingmar! Of course!" And now he saw that the stone bearing the name "Anderson" was a generic monument, whereas the two smaller shafts marked actual graves. Carved on the one to the left of the monument was "I.A. 1873-1933," and on the other, "T.N. 1897-1939."

"That's odd," Jon said. "Just initials. Who's 'T.N.?'"

"I don't know, but *zat*, darlink, is where you dig!"

When he looked at her questioningly, she shrugged. "I suppose I tell you. Yelena had a number of letters from a man named Vaino—which I burned. Does zat make me a bad girl?" She laughed nervously, glancing beyond the torches at the woods. "Zis Vaino person made it quite clear Yelena came to Ingmar's burial service in 1939 and brought ze Imperial Eggs."

When Jon did not reply she said, "You must get the rest of your zings from ze car."

As he returned for a shovel and the other items he had purchased, Jon felt an intense unease, not to be accounted for by the immediate prospect of heavy labor. Xenia's silly gun, his frustration over Georgia, and even Violet's disappearance doubtless contributed. But there was some cause more profound, more unchanging, more real. Perhaps it had to do with the suspended quiet of the place, as if behind each tree a watching animal or spirit held its breath.

"How lonk will it take?" Xenia inquired, when he came back to the monuments. She was careful to stand well out of his reach, beyond any swing of his shovel.

"Mm. At least two hours. Maybe three. It depends how deep they're buried." Pulling on gloves, he made the first thrust of the shovel into the soft, loamy soil. He used his foot to drive it deeper, then raised the first load of grassy earth and tossed it to the side. Thus he began opening the grave.

He worked steadily, clearing out the top nine inches of earth without much awareness of Xenia, who ensconced herself beyond the foot of the grave. She sat on the ground, her handbag and canvas sack nearby, the gun in her right hand. From time to time she bit into an apple.

Jon paused to remove his coat and wipe the sweat from his brow. "Got any beer in that sack?" he asked.

"Wine. And some Cokes."

"Make it a Coke." He watched how she mismanaged the gun in reaching for the Coke. "Thanks." He drank quickly and resumed his work.

Although Jon was silent, she chatted, intermittently, once bringing up the mysterious occupant of the grave and wondering if Ingmar might have been a bigamist. But more often she was silent, and the only sounds were of spade digging into earth, of wind moaning through the forest, of Xenia biting into the apple. Jon remained silent and continued digging, down to almost three feet. Then he stopped, rose up, and dropped his shovel at the side of the deepening hole. One step brought him out, whereupon he asked Xenia, "How about another Coke? This is hot work." Taking off the gloves, he began unbuttoning his shirt.

She tensed when he stepped from the excavation, but relaxed following his request. Delving into the sack, she briefly looked away from him. Prepared to toss the Coke to him, she looked up, but he was already upon her. The gun went off harmlessly into the earth as he wrenched it away. In a rage, she bit him on the shoulder and pounded on his back, but he brushed her off roughly and soon stood over her, the gun in his hand.

"Bastard!" she exclaimed breathlessly. "You've ruined it!" She was on her back in the grass, propped up on her elbows. "*Merde!*"

For a moment he held the gun on her, then put on the safety catch and pocketed it. "I'm going to tie you up," he announced, reaching down for her. She tried to get away, but he speedily got her under control with an arm lock.

"Bastard!" she repeated, tears of pain and frustration in her eyes.

"Be still!" he cautioned, as she tried to kick him with her spiked heels. He tightened his hold cruelly, eliciting a loud gasp. "Quiet, damn you!" he growled, for he had heard a sound, the snap of a twig, in the woods. "Someone's out there!"

She ceased struggling, and they both listened. The silence seemed absolute, but for her rasping breath and a lone, distant car. Then a twig snapped beyond the circle of light cast by the torches. Drawing Xenia with him, holding her as a shield, he retreated from the sound.

Suddenly a voice said, "Stop right there, if you please."

Jon switched his hold on Xenia to the left hand and reached for the gun in his pocket.

But now, from behind them, another voice ordered, "Don't move, Cowboy!" and Jon froze, for the thing pressing into his back felt like the muzzle of a large weapon, more than likely a shotgun.

CHAPTER 25

▼

Two men, one of them holding a handgun, walked into the torchlight in front of Jon and Xenia. The unarmed man was older and dressed far more elegantly than one might expect in a bucolic setting. "Let the woman go," he said to Jon, and the other pulled Xenia away. He continued in an ironic tone, "May I introduce myself, Mr. Olsen. I'm Felix Ratliff. Excuse me if I don't shake your hand." He chuckled humorlessly.

Jon registered little surprise. "I figured you would be mixed up in this somehow." In spite of the gun at his back, he added, "But tell me, isn't your kind usually deserting ships rather than joining them at such a late hour?"

Ratliff pretended not to notice the word play. "I've been on this ship, as you call it, a little longer than you may realize." When Jon did not respond, he added, "So you're the man who drove Mrs. Beech back to Kentucky." He looked Jon up and down. "I can't say that I understand her reaction."

Meanwhile the individual who most concerned Jon—the man behind him with the shotgun—began frisking him with his free hand. There was no hiding the gun in his pocket, of course, and soon he was again disarmed. As the frisk proceeded, he recognized the man holding

Xenia as the anonymous character he had noticed at the airport and in the bar.

"Hold her tight," Ratliff said to the man with Xenia. He turned to Jon. "And you, sir, may continue to dig." He indicated the partially opened grave.

Jon glanced over his shoulder at the man behind, who forced him forward with little jabs of the shotgun into his back. The glance had revealed Xenia's gun now bulging in his jacket pocket. Cautiously Jon moved to the grave, taking as much time as possible while his mind whirled. He knew he had either to capitulate to Ratliff now, hoping for an opportunity to somehow turn the tables later, or to strike immediately, while one of his men—the only other with a weapon—was occupied with Xenia. He made his decision immediately. "I'd like a Coke," he said, wiping his brow. "This is exhausting work."

"Oh, yes. The occasion earlier for such dramatics," observed Ratliff. He snapped his fingers, and the man holding Xenia bent to reach into her canvas sack.

At that, apparently seeing her future slipping away, Xenia screamed like a bobcat and managed to tear herself from his lax grip. He grappled with her and she threw herself upon the sack, dragging him with her. When his companion rushed over to help, Jon picked up the shovel and in one stride whacked him on the head. He groaned heavily and dropped unconscious to the ground, the shotgun pinned beneath him. Jon then stepped toward Ratliff, the shovel raised threateningly.

Suddenly, there came the loud report of a gun from the woods. Everybody in the circle of light stopped, a tableaux of action figures seemingly frozen in time. At the very edge of the circle, the mustachioed youth stood, his face obscured by the hat, but his grasp of a blued Magnum totally professional.

Ratliff stood facing Jon, his hands raised above his face as though to ward off a blow. The anonymous man sat perfectly still, his hands high in the air in surrender. Beside him, Xenia clutched the sack to her body as if to the death. Jon dropped the shovel and raised his hands at the sight of the Magnum.

The next event completely befuddled Jon and Xenia. Into the torch-light, from behind the figure that had fired the gun, marched Aunt Violet, as though on a charger! And moving into her place was a distinguished looking elderly gentleman, who glided silently out of the shadows and stopped near the armed youth.

"Well!" Violet declared, obviously loving her entrance, "We seem to've managed quite nicely! Oh, don't look so startled, Jon! It's out of character!"

"Cousin Violet!" exclaimed Xenia, equally amazed, and still hoarding the sack.

"I don't know why I'm shocking everybody," Violet said a bit testily, probably to hide her delight at the fact. "Jon, shouldn't you tie up these men? And please do something about all these guns; it looks like an armed insurrection!"

Jon moved at once to do her bidding, binding the three men hand and foot with plumber's tape, then placing the guns in the canvas bag, which he moved a safe distance from Xenia. As he went about his tasks, he glanced toward the shadows in an effort to see the Magnum's owner and get a better look at the elderly man. Extra-ordinarily unwavering, the weapon loomed larger than ever in the moonlight. Its wielder, however, remained essentially concealed. Jon noted that Felix Ratliff remained silent as well as motionless during this procedure, apparently also attempting to identify the hero in the shadows.

Xenia, seemingly oblivious to her villainous role in the plot, turned to Violet and exclaimed, "Darlink! How did you find us!"

"Some of us are a little more capable of trailing people than your husband." Violet's dark eyes sparkled in the torchlight.

"What do you mean!"

"He's incompetent."

"You mean Rudi?"

"Do you have another husband?" she asked, as if she enjoyed the impertinence.

"What a zink to say!"

Now Jon, finishing with the nondescript man, at last found words. "Where *is* Rudi, Aunt Violet? And who's your companion?" Again he gazed toward the Magnum.

"Rudi's still changing a tire in the dark somewhere, I imagine. As for your second question, shouldn't we take care of these criminals first," she informed him.

"Well, they're pretty well trussed up. Do you want me to toss them into the grave?" For the first time in several days, he laughed out loud.

All this time Violet's mysterious hired gun stayed silently in the shadows, but now the voice behind the Magnum said, "Tie the woman, too!"

Violet watched Xenia and Jon as they reacted to the words. For Xenia, the response was alarm and disbelief, followed by a screech and a protest. For Jon, it was a startle and then a concentrated stare toward the Magnum.

"Do it, Jon!" commanded the voice. "Xenia's as guilty as the others."

He carried out the order, not without some difficulty, for of course he at once recognized the youth's voice. Xenia fought and scratched and wheedled and spat. But in the end, he trussed her up like the others, whereupon she burst into tears and cried, "You've ruined it!"

"I'm sorry," he said, not convincingly.

"You're not! Not in the least," she cried

Violet said, "Leave her!" Then to her nephew, in a much kinder tone, "Come with me." So he followed her to the edge of light and darkness, to where Anna Nygaard stood, holstering the Magnum.

"So it *is* you!" he marveled, his mind in a whirl, and yet he had pause to smile, not so much at the male attire as at the curving mustache.

Anna turned to the elegant old man standing near her. "Jon Olsen, I'd like you to meet Jäger Vaino, long-time friend and confidante of Yelena Anderson. They lived near each other on Bygdøy for many years. Mr. Vaino was of inestimable help getting us here tonight. But for his assistance, you might still be trying to get the jump on Ratliff and his cronies."

"Then I do indeed owe him a debt," Jon said graciously, and shook hands with the elderly man, who had a grip of steel.

"We must find the Eggs and leave," Anna said, very businesslike suddenly. "How much longer to dig, Jon?"

He was taken aback, but did not show it. "An hour, maybe."

"And if I help?"

"Less."

"We've brought a shovel," she informed him.

"What about the prisoners?"

"Violet can watch them."

He looked at his aunt. "She can't shoot."

"Well, *they* don't know that," said Violet gamely. "Besides, Mr. Vaino can help me. Between the two of us, I daresay they won't try anything."

Anna said, her voice low, "It's important I'm not recognized—by Ratliff *or* his agents," and pulled the wide brim of her hat farther down over her eyes. "Could you tie them behind those big trees over there?"

"Sure he said," smiling. She was very elegantly and theatrically dressed, and Jon suddenly remembered.

"You were on the plane!"

"Of course."

He laughed delightedly, then walked back to where the prisoners lay. He unceremoniously dragged them one by one to nearby trees, then wrapped plumber's tape around them and the base of the trees facing away from the grave site. Always the gentleman, he carried Xenia rather than dragged her, and was cursed for his efforts.

On the way to the lighted area around the grave, Jon handed Violet the little automatic with a warning about the safety. She accepted gingerly, holding it at arms length. Vaino requested the shotgun, with the observation that he had shot more than one brace of ducks in his day. Thus armed, they sat down a few yards from the prisoners and waited.

At the grave site, Anna leaned on a shovel, awaiting his arrival. Her moustache made him smile again. Stooping and picking up his gloves, he offered them to her.

"They're just a tad big, Jon," she said, and whipped a pair of driving gloves from her pants pocket.

While she pulled on the gloves, Jon said, "If you were hoping to travel incognito, that outfit was a strange choice." He smiled again at the mustache and hat.

"It's the only thing I could find in my size on such short notice," she said, pulling off the hat and tossing it aside, allowing her hair to cascade to her shoulders. "The costume shop had nothing but ballroom gowns, nun's habits, and French maid outfits. None seemed quite appropriate for my purposes." He thought he glimpsed the hint of a smile, but suddenly she was all business again. "Perhaps we should begin."

Rather than bend immediately to the task, he thought for a moment then announced he had a plan. The idea was for him to shovel out the grave and for her to toss the soil farther as needed to keep it from tumbling back into the pit again. He had already reached a depth that made it difficult to throw the dirt out beyond the edge. Anna agreed that this, indeed, would be the most sensible approach, given the depth they would have to excavate.

As he prepared to jump into the grave, she stopped him with the almost whispered words, "This reminds me of pictures of the Four Brothers site."

The term sounded familiar, and Jon asked her what she meant.

"The mineshaft into which the remains of the Tsar and his family were thrown lay on a tract of land called the Four Brothers. It was much like this," she murmured, "a meadow, pines, stumps, a small clearing. Of course, it was a much bigger hole."

Jon blocked the light from the torches and looked beyond at the meadow in the moonlight, lying perhaps not so smooth, not so placid as one might like to think. God alone knew what was beneath the rich soil of the meadow. Returning his gaze to her, he asked, "And what does it mean in relation to us right here, right now?"

"I know who is buried in this grave," she announced in somber tones. When Jon did not respond, she said, "Shall we begin?"

He leaped down into the dark, dank earth.

CHAPTER 26

▼

In the moonlight, augmented by the torches, the excavation deepened to forty inches, to four feet, to five feet. As Jon's work grew more strenuous and he began to tire, the interval between shovelfuls gradually and imperceptibly lengthened. He perspired freely, so that Anna more frequently handed cups of water from the jug she had provided.

At such times, they talked briefly, she kneeling or squatting at the side of the excavation. In this mode he learned details about the murder of the Tsar, about the competition for Yelena's Imperial Eggs, about the increasing ambiguity of his relationship to Anna. Unfamiliar thoughts swirled in his mind, like the chips in a French glass paperweight.

"Why is Jäger Vaino helping us?" Jon asked at one point.

"Because he likes me." She looked at him mock-coquettishly, but when he did not take the bait, she became businesslike again. "Mr. Vaino never really approved of Yelena's Eggs being buried here. He was afraid of exactly this kind of thing happening, only with bulldozers and steam shovels and television cameras. That's why he agreed to help us. He wants them out of here once and for all. And he wants a relative of Yelena's to have them rather than a governmental agency such as the Soviet KGB."

Or *your* agency, Jon guessed. Although he did not say so, he deduced that Anna was an intelligence officer—perhaps with the Central Intelligence Agency or with one of the military branches. There were all the signs: the Embassy connection, her handling of the Magnum, the disguise, her ease with their extralegal situation. Equally telling were the informative anecdotes, the implied admissions. The Imperial Eggs must not find their way to the Soviets via Felix Ratliff, she said. Did Jon not know the Kremlin collection was about to be surpassed? The Russians would go to almost any lengths to prevent such a national disgrace, would put some of their best people on it. And yes, the man guarded by Violet was indeed Ratliff, who represented the Soviets in this affair. His presence in the meadow was testament to the Eggs' importance.

And then she told him of Rudi's scheme to cheat the world, to cheat anybody and everybody—except Rudi's scheme was thwarted by Xenia's theft of the counterfeit eggs, which Jon doubtless would find if he opened her precious canvas sack. Of course, Rudi had done nothing illegal as yet. He had merely fabricated three eggs in the style of Faberge. He could still come out well for a man who didn't even notice when someone tampered with his tires. He could end up with half the real Eggs, and be free of Xenia to boot. Violet had every intention of sharing the inheritance with Rudi, in spite of his malevolent plan to defraud her.

Jon wondered what would happen to Xenia, when all was finished here, and Anna answered, "You'll drop her off on the highway as you leave Switzerland."

"*I* will?"

"It's better than she deserves. What do you think she planned to do with you after she secured the Eggs?"

"I hadn't thought that far ahead," he admitted. "I was planning to use the Eggs to learn what they had done with Aunt Violet."

"Now you won't need to. Violet and I'll be across the border, with the Eggs."

"Oh, *will* you?"

"Certainly. I'll play my 'diplomatic immunity' card. Otherwise, the thrifty Swiss will find a way to charge us a fee, at the very least. They might even impound the Eggs." And she went on to say that he must make his own escape fast, that otherwise he would be held, perhaps indefinitely. "You'll be persona non grata anywhere the Soviets have influence, Jon."

"What about Ratliff and his men?" Jon asked, not particularly concerned with Soviet opinion of himself. "What happens to them?"

"I'll arrange for somebody from Russian intelligence to pick them up—anonymously, of course. This is part of the little game we play at the embassy. We don't go around shooting each other nowadays, but we do love to embarrass our opponents, to humiliate them. After this little escapade, Felix Ratliff will never again be quite the force he was in Russian intelligence. His shooting star went 'poof!' tonight."

That pleased Jon for some reason. But how did she know all this, he inquired. How did she know these things about the law and Rudi and Felix Ratliff?

Oh, she knew, she made a point of knowing things: of looking up the law, of befriending Violet, of reading Yelena's mail, of following Rudi and Xenia. It was all part of the service of your friendly embassy.

Mentally, he added to her list the activity of cultivating Jon Olsen, and he at once felt a vague distress, or perhaps not so vague. It was not a matter of pride, of anger at being fooled. No, not so petty as that. It was rather a feeling of loss, of indefinite and permanent loss, such as one sometimes has for yesterday.

He knew now that her "obsession" with him, so inexplicable, was a staged affair. It had never truly existed—a thing he ought to have known. And *did* know, intuitively, but had come to disregard as he grew to enjoy the attention, as he became fond of Anna—the false Anna, now vanished forever.

And the night seemed to him beautiful but oppressive, as that summer night at the Four Brothers may have been, with the fires and the corpses. Just as here. And Death hovered over their activity, in its most awesome form as the Bringer of the End of Things. Whoever lay buried beneath Jon's spade was no more revivable than one's most cherished dreams.

CHAPTER 27

▼

Beyond six feet, Jon's shovel struck something harder than the earth. Anna heard the sound and came to the edge of the pit. "The coffin!" she whispered, and drew in her breath. He began scooping away the layer of soil above the object. She asked if he could see, and he reported it looked like metal, possibly wood with metal.

Anna brought one of the torches closer. Every pass of the shovel scraped against the coffin now. "Can you see? Is there writing?" she asked.

"I think so."

The next moment she was in the pit with him. "Where? Where do you see writing?" And, pulling a small flashlight from her waistband, she directed it downwards. "Ah!"

"It's Cyrillic, isn't it?"

"Yes," she breathed, and squatted to brush away the soil. "Yes, yes! A double eagle!" Then she read slowly, solemnly, "'Tatiana Nicholayevna.' Ah!"

"The Tsar's daughter?" he asked incredulously, not really believing what she said. "I was so worried it would be Yelena."

She looked at him oddly. "Yelena's up there, in an urn." She pointed to the darkness beyond the meadow, to the nearby hills.

"She's *where?*"

"In Vaino's house. He had her cremated shortly after she died on Bygdøy, then brought her ashes with him to Switzerland. He's debating burying her in Oslo, with his own ashes—or spreading them here on the meadow."

"How do you know all this?"

"We had a nice long visit the other day. He told me everything."

"You're amazing!" he said. "Yet you chose not to tell us anything."

"When did I have a chance?" she countered. "After I rescued your aunt from Wally Macleod, I had to act fast. I hid her at the embassy."

"So *that's* where she was! I was worried sick."

"Wally was one of Ratliff's temporary hires—a bad one as it turned out. The ninny was supposed to tail you and keep tabs on Violet. But he and Rudi decided to go into business for themselves, to kidnap Violet and keep you busy searching for her." She laughed quietly. "The best thing that ever happened to Wally was crossing swords with me. The headache I left him with was nothing compared to what Ratliff would have done when he found out."

While she talked, Jon continued to shovel dirt away from the perimeter of the coffin. He looked again at Tatiana's crest. "I still can't believe this," he said. "After all, the history books say the Tsar's family were all killed, chopped into bits, dipped in acid, burned, then thrown down a mineshaft in the sector of the Four Brothers."

"Yes, yes! But Mannerheim rescued her, you see. The Germans, Vaino, your cousin Ingmar—they were all part of it. Somehow they saved Tatiana, to bring her here. Vaino wouldn't tell me how—just that they did. They may have killed a few people along the way." She said these things in a low voice while looking up at him.

Jon was finding it difficult to take in, to accept. She seemed to sense that. Grasping the shovel to help herself rise, she faced him in the grave, so deep that only he could see above it. She said quietly, "Mannerheim was the only victorious White Russian in the end, and the Tsarina's people were Germans." Then, as he still looked at her skeptically, she went on, "Mannerheim sent the men to save her—Vaino,

Ingmar, the others. They were all trained by Germans. Either they came too late to save the rest of the family, or they triggered the executions by their success with Tatiana. I don't know which."

They gazed at one another, to the sounds of the flickering torches—now burning lower—and the wind sighing in the firs. Was it possible events had occurred so differently than history had recorded? Did the course of empires sometimes turn on little things like timing, on details forever lost in the past? Were the edifices of mankind that fragile?

He said at last, "You guessed all along who was buried here, right?"

She nodded. "Yes. I wasn't positive, of course, until Vaino verified it. Sometimes the job requires as much guesswork as footwork."

He studied her face—for what, he was not sure. Really, even wearing the silly, pasted mustache, she was delicious in a frosted drink kind of way. The thought made him smile.

At that, her gaze actually wavered, and she even looked away. "Violet," she suddenly murmured, "Violet should see. I'll get her." She struggled to climb out of the hole, and Jon hoisted her to the edge, a mere feather in his hands.

At the top, on her feet, she turned to peer down at him, perhaps shocked at how easily he had lifted her. Then she was gone.

Once again he worked, this time removing the remnants of dirt covering the coffin and clearing it several inches below the level of the lid. He had barely completed this task when Anna returned, Aunt Violet in tow.

"Here we are," Anna said. "Vaino is watching the prisoners."

"Did they give you any trouble?" he asked his Aunt. Her big, black eyes were wide, and Jon guessed Anna had informed her that Tatiana was buried there.

"Not at all," she said, almost proudly. "Two of them are fast asleep. Mr. Ratliff spent most of the time offering us inducements to release him." She laughed delightedly. "He's not terribly fond of you at the moment, Jon. Or me, for that matter. And he's dying to know who Anna is."

Jon wanted to hear more, but he had completed the digging and was ready for the next stage. "Give me the crowbar, will you," he said to Anna. While they watched from above, he sank to his knees in the small space he had made between earth wall and coffin. After trying the lid with the crowbar he said, "This is going to be easy. There's not much left of the wood." He stopped for a moment and looked up at Anna. The moment seemed fraught with tension. "Want to join me for the grand opening?"

"Puns are the lowest form of humor, Jon," she said, clambering into the grave, torch in hand. In spite of her protest, he thought he saw the glimmer of a smile.

Violet seemed not to have heard. "The Grand Duchess!" she muttered. "Tatiana Nicholayevna! What if Xenia was right? What if she is Tatiana's granddaughter?"

"That silly story of hers doesn't prove a thing," Anna scoffed.

"But it keeps alive the possibility," Violet pointed out. "It means, it conceivably could be."

"I'm afraid that's a very romantic view."

"The past *is* romantic. The future, too. It's only the present that's dull," Violet said.

"If you find this particular moment dull, Aunt Violet, you're a better man than I!" muttered Jon. "Now, ladies, can we break up this historical overview and pry open the coffin? I could have sworn that's why we're here!"

Again his words seemed to fly over his aunt's head, for she continued to say, "The Grand Duchess!" And, "Poor Xenia! She will never really know!"

As Anna moved the torch closer, Jon began to pry at the lid, his muscles rippling, his moist skin shining in the hellish light. Then came a moment when resistance ceased, when he slid the panel from the coffin to reveal a black velvet shroud stretching its entire length. Beneath the tattered shroud was the clear, bony outline of a skeleton, the feet sticking out grotesquely. But it was not the shroud or the skeleton that drew their eyes; what most intrigued them were seven small, moldering boxes resting at the coffin's side.

Violet gasped and Anna rose from her knees, perhaps to put psychic distance between the coffin, herself, and the end of their quest. Jon, all business as usual, neither looked up nor paused, but raised each box gingerly from its resting place and handed it to Anna. She in turn surrendered the boxes to Violet, standing at the edge of the grave.

"What I don't quite understand," said Jon, handing the final box to Anna, is why Yelena decided to bury the Eggs with Tatiana. They could have made her a wealthy woman."

"Oh, I understand completely," said Violet, placing the box near the brightest torch. "Yelena always insisted on doing the right thing. She felt the Eggs belonged to the Tsar's family, and this was the perfect way to guarantee they remained with them forever."

Anna appeared skeptical, but she said nothing as she helped Jon climb from the grave. "Poor thing," she said softly, "you must be exhausted."

"I think I have just enough energy to examine the Eggs," he grinned, and followed her to the spot Violet had selected for the viewing.

They opened the boxes, one by one, onto another world. It was a world of beauty and reflected light, of ballrooms on snowy nights, of crystal chandeliers and enameled chanticleers, a world unconcerned with fission, fusion, vulgar tastes, and vulgar feelings. It was a world now gone, but bits of it lay encapsulated in these, its exquisite legacies.

After long moments of admiring that other world, Jon loaded the boxes onto the ladies' arms, whereupon they carried them gingerly to their car.

Thus left alone, he carefully replaced the coffin lid, hammered it down, and then threw his tools to the surface above. With an effort, he lifted himself from the pit and, after pausing to arch his back and otherwise flex his weary muscles, began refilling the grave.

In a little while, Anna came back. She stood close by, staring, seemingly transfixed by the play of moonlight on his smoothly muscled torso as he worked. He stopped for a moment and looked at her, the ridiculous mustache now gone from her lovely face. Moonlight and flames danced in her hair as she stepped close to him. Then, much to his consternation, she placed her hands on his chest, stood on tiptoe, and gave him a soft, lingering kiss. It was not the kiss of someone playing a role. It was a kiss filled with promise, a kiss that made his head reel and his heart skip a beat.

What might finally come of that kiss, Jon could only guess.

0-595-66079-7

Printed in the United States
16913LVS00001B/148